ALSO BY

- *FREEDOM COLORADO SERIES:*

- Baked with Love

- Playing for Keeps

- Sheriff's Convenient Bride

- Daddy's Second Chance

- The Scars Within

- Guarding her Heart

- *PHOENIX SECURITY SERIES:*

- Hidden Desires

- Uncovering her Secrets

- *RIPPERS' MC SERIES*

- Undertaker's Match

- Christmas Boyfriend

- Hawk's Redemption

- Fury's Lady

- Rider's Claim

- ***Naughty Professors Series***

- Teacher's Pet

Cover Artist: Michelle Sewell with RLS Images, Graphics & Design

Cover photographer: Jane Ashley Converse

Model: Kevin R. Davis

FALLING FOR FANG

STEPHANIE WEBB DILLON

1

Fang

I had finally convinced Cara Daniels to go out with me and then one of the freaking strippers had to show up and ruin things. I'm not a saint and I haven't lived like a monk all these years. I just normally take care of my needs discreetly. Brandi was one of the strippers at Trixie's and I had sex with her once or twice before I took over as manager of the club. After that I didn't touch any of them. I don't shit where I eat. I was going to find out who brought Brandi to my sister's wedding and then I was going to beat their ass. I stalked across the yard past the guests until I got to the security building. I walked in and the pledge looked startled.

"What's your name, pledge?" I demanded more than asked as he looked me in the eye. He stood up and stuck out his hand.

"I'm Remy, your name is Fang, right?" he asked as he looked me in the eye. Yeah, I think this kid would do just fine.

"Right, I want to know who let the stripper into my sisters' wedding. I want to fucking know right now." I growled at him, still pissed about my date being ruined. To the guys' credit, he didn't hesitate to pull up the footage of the guests arriving. We watched for a minute before a string of French sounding curses flew from Remy's mouth.

"Damn, that's my brother Luke. He has been talking about this girl he met at the club. I didn't realize it was one of the strippers. I'm sure he didn't know you had an issue with her." Remy said frustrated as hell. "Please don't kick him out, if you tell him he will never do it again. The Rippers mean more to him than that piece of ass who was obviously using him."

"He is going to get put through some paces but no, we won't boot him for this." I said running my hand through my hair. "Let him know that he needs to see me at the club tomorrow night and don't tell him what it's about. I have to go do damage control."

"Sure thing." Remy said as he took his seat back behind the cameras. I nodded and left.

I got my truck and took off toward the shelter. I knew that's where she would end up. I didn't want to take my bike because she wasn't dressed to ride. She had an apartment, but she spent ninety percent of her time at her shelter and clinic. My girl loved animals. She may not have figured it out yet, but she is mine. I stopped by and grabbed her favorite coffee and some of her favorite chocolate. Pulling up I didn't see her car. We were going to talk this time instead of her running off in a fit. I walked into the shelter door and was pissed to realize that it was open when she was alone here. That wouldn't do at all. Heading back toward the kennels I found her on the floor in her pretty dress with a couple of kittens in her lap. She was crying and looked so sad it ripped my heart out. When I stepped in front of the door to the kennel, she looked up at me and her face turned cold.

"Get the fuck out." She screamed at me. "I don't want you here. Go back to your whore."

"She is not mine and I am going to get the chance to defend myself. You can sit there and listen quietly, or I'll put you over my shoulder and take you to your office." I said firmly. Her eyes glittered with anger and tears. She stroked the kitten still in her lap and looked down. I sighed and sat down on the floor beside her.

"Look kitten, I am not a saint. I have not lived like a monk all these years. Raising Katherine, I took care of my needs away from home. Yes, I had sex with Brandi a couple of times, but it was before I started working there as a manager. I have not touched any of them since, it's been over six months. It was just sex, there were no feelings involved, she never came to my home or my room at the clubhouse. I hadn't met anyone that I wanted to get to know on a serious level until I saw you. We usually don't let sweet butts and club whores hang around during family events, she conned one of the pledges into bringing her as his date. I'm sorry she upset you. She means nothing to me. She knew the score. I never led her on." I told her as I watched her reactions. I hoped she would give me a chance. I stood up and brushed off my pants.

Cara put the kittens back in the box they slept in and stood up. She had worn sandals to the wedding, so she slipped those back on and walked past me out of the kennel. I followed her and waited for her to close the door.

"Are you hungry?" I asked her as she looked up at me. She started to speak and then her stomach growled making both of us laugh. She blushed. "I guess that's my answer. Can I take you out to get some dinner?"

"I'd like that, I'm too embarrassed to go back to the reception after running out like that." She blushed. "My purse is in the office."

I followed her to her office so she could get her purse and lock up the shelter. I opened the door and then helped her into my truck. After closing her door, I went around to the driver's side to get in.

"What would you like to eat?" I asked her. "Your choice kitten, whatever you want."

"Can we just grab some pizza and go to my place?" she asked me. "I'd really like to change into something more comfortable. I'm not much of a dress person."

"Sure, why don't we go to your place and order it to be delivered." I suggested to her. She smiled at me and nodded. I pulled up behind her car in her driveway and parked. "Don't open that door."

I helped her out of the truck and then walked her to the door. She opened it up and I followed her inside. Her two dogs came bounding over to her. They were mutts, one was a small breed mix and the other medium.

"They don't bite, I'll be right back." She said as she disappeared into her bedroom. She came out a few minutes later in some leggings and a loose-fitting sweatshirt. Her blonde bob was still loose, and she looked just as lovely as she had in the dress. I had been courting her for a few weeks now. Bringing her breakfast and dinner some nights as well. She had a habit of working too many hours. Cara was about five feet six inches which was still a good half foot shorter than me. She had beautiful blonde hair, tanned skin likely from working outside with the animals so much. She was curvy and soft the way a woman was meant to be. There wasn't anything I didn't like about her.

2

C^{ara}

I still could not believe that Fang was in my apartment. I walked back into the living room to find him sitting on the floor with my dogs. They were both fighting for his attention. He noticed the second I walked back into the room. His eyes heated as he looked over me. I didn't know what he saw because I was a lot heavier than that woman that came to find him. I was thick, I always have been, and I have just learned to deal with it. I have tried to workout, diet and nothing really works. I might lose down to a size twelve for a few months but then it all comes back. What can I say? I like food. There this man was playing with my dogs, tall, handsome, with a salt and peppered beard. I knew he was in his middle to late thirties and that he had been a part of the Rippers for most of his adult life. I got the skinny from my best friend Sophie. She was married to Gears. I had seen him at several barbeques and parties, but I avoided him for the most part.

I had noticed him months ago and I found him to be very attractive. He was always a gentleman around me, and he was good with animals as well as kids. He had started bringing me things a few weeks ago. He brought me breakfast a few times and stopped off with lunch. He will bring me coffee. Just little thoughtful things. It's cute, like old fashioned courting. It makes me smile the rest of the day when I get to see him. I realized I was lost in my own thoughts when I noticed his eyebrow raised.

"Have you ordered yet?" I asked him as I sat on the couch. I reached down and picked Kirk up off the floor. He was my snuggle pup. Spock was a bit older and didn't like to be held much.

"I was waiting to see what you like?" he asked me with a smile. "What are their names?"

"The old spaniel mix beside you is Spock and the one in my lap is Kirk." I said, waiting for his reaction. His eyes sparkled with amusement. "Yes, I'm a Star Trek geek."

"I love Star Trek. We can talk about our favorite genres after I order dinner. What would you like on your pizza?" he asked me.

"No onions, mushrooms or anchovies but otherwise I don't care." I told him.

Pulling out his phone, Fang placed the order and then put his phone down. He got up and stretched then sat down on the couch beside me. I wanted nothing more than to scoot closer. He smelled so good. The cologne was something fresh and citrusy. He had sexy tattoos on his arms and the prettiest blue eyes. I kept Kirk close so I wouldn't give in to the urge.

"What would you like to watch?" I asked him as I handed him the remote. "I have a selection of DVDs in the tv cabinet."

"Whatever you want to watch is fine with me. Looks like you may have good taste." He winked as he settled onto the couch. I put in one of my favorites, Star Trek Generations. "Good choice."

The doorbell rang about 20 minutes later, so I paused the movie while Fang went to pay for the pizza. He found some plates and put a few slices on each then fixed us both some ice water.

"Let's eat at the table then we can finish the movie. The boys will try to steal our food if we eat on the couch." I suggested as I got up and washed my hands. We both sat down and started to eat. I noticed that he got pepperoni, sausage and olives. "My favorite." I bit into it and moaned at the taste. I had not had pizza in a while. All my extra money went to the shelter animals. I usually packed a pb and j for lunch and mostly drank water. This was a treat.

"While I hate that the first part of our date got ruined, I'm glad that I get to be alone with you." Fang said as he wiped the corner of my mouth with his thumb and sucked it clean. I could feel my face flush again. We ate in silence then I cleaned up our plates and placed the leftovers in the fridge. We took our drinks to the living area and sat back down on the couch. He sat on the end, slipped off his boots and leaned back with his arm stretched over the back of the couch. I decided what the hell and curled up close to him pulling the blanket off the back of the couch to cover my legs with. Turning the movie back on he wrapped his arm around me, and we watched the rest of the movie cuddled up. He was so warm and cozy I must have fallen asleep because I felt myself being lifted into his arms and carried. He put me in my bed and covered me up. I felt him press a kiss to my head before succumbing to sleep.

I woke up to my phone buzzing beside the bed. I jumped up and looked at the clock. It was seven thirty in the morning. I had not slept that long in ages. I got up and showered, dressed and fixed my thermos of coffee. Beside the coffee maker was a note.

Kitten,

You were sleeping so soundly I didn't have the heart to wake you. I'd like to see you again tonight. I'll call you around lunch to see if we can make plans.

Yours,

Fang

Smiling ear to ear, I fed the boys and let them outside before heading into the shelter. I took them with me today. They liked to play, and I had beds in my office for them when I was doing paperwork. I hated to leave them at home all day.

We pulled up to the building and headed inside. I put the boys in the playroom with some dog toys and went to feed the animals. I didn't have many clinic appointments today unless there was an emergency. The morning went by quickly, between feeding the animals, letting them out to play as well as getting some exercise and cleaning their kennels. I tried to give them as much attention as I could. I will be having an open adoption day next Saturday. I did that once a month to try and find homes for as many as I could. We were a no kill shelter. I took as many as I could handle. It always broke my heart if I had to turn anyone away. I was heading to my office to eat my sandwich when I heard my phone beep. I looked down and saw a message from Fang. He was telling me that he would like to cook me dinner if I was up to it tonight or we could go out. I really enjoyed having him to myself last night but maybe it was too forward to have him at my house two nights in a row. I sent him a message back.

Me: Dinner out sounds nice. I can be ready by five.

Fang: I'll be at your house at five on the dot.

I put the phone on my desk and sat down to do the schedule for the next pay period. I only had an assistant currently. The others were volunteers that gave me their availability and I scheduled around it. They were a blessing because I just couldn't afford to pay everyone.

After I went through and checked on the animals getting them settled. I put leashes on Spock and Kirk so we could go home. I needed to shower and get ready for my date. Sophie and I didn't get our weekly breakfast yesterday because of the wedding but she would be calling me tomorrow at lunch for an update. I had a lot to tell her.

I pulled into my driveway and let the boys do their business before going inside and getting ready for our date. After a quick shower, I found a pair of my favorite jeans and a long sleeve sweatshirt along with a pair of leather boots that were knee high. I used my round brush to smooth my hair as I dried it. Putting on just a little makeup I was ready. I glanced at my watch, and it was four fifty.

3

Fang

Going home the night before had really sucked but I could tell that Cara was exhausted. I don't know how long I just sat there and enjoyed having her curled up to me. She was so sweet and snuggly when she was sleepy. I know she works too much so I just decided to put her to bed and try to see her tonight.

After sending the message about dinner and getting the response I was happy as a clam. I wanted her on the back of my bike again, so I decided to take that with the extra helmet I had for Katherine when she was younger. I had to work later tonight but not until ten, so I slept later this morning. I looked around my room at the clubhouse and wondered about having a place built. I had given our old house to Katherine and Rider as a wedding gift. Now I didn't really have a place to bring Cara except the clubhouse. That was ok sometimes, but not when there were parties going on. Since I didn't have to pick her up for another couple of hours I decided to hang in the common area. It was a Sunday afternoon so it should be fairly quiet. Except for the guys watching sports. I looked around and didn't see anyone, so I sat down and turned on an old boxing match. Just some background noise while I thought about how I was going to deal with Luke at the club later and the talk I was going to have with Brandi. I really didn't want to deal with her.

I guess I could fire her, but she was a good dancer and a favorite of our regulars. I'd give her a chance to straighten up. Luke needed to understand the rules of the compound. We were going to have a chat. I heard Axle and Blade come in the back door. Most of the single guys ate here. Lillian fixed casseroles and things that froze and reheat well for the single guys. She was a sweetheart. We also grilled a lot since there were several guys and we could eat a lot.

"Hey Fang, did you get to catch up with the cute vet after Brandi made her scene yesterday?" Blade asked. I would have snapped at him except I was in too good of a mood, and he wasn't being facetious but sounded genuine.

"Yeah, we had dinner and watched a movie at her place. I'm taking her to dinner tonight." I told them, smiling. Axle had a funny look on his face and then came over to where I was sitting.

"I know you were used to living on your own. Cara is welcome here anytime you know. We can also look at building a house for you on one of the vacant lots on the property. Just let me know." Axle said as he sipped a beer.

"Thanks, I'm thinking about it." I told him as I checked the time. I had a little over an hour before I could pick her up. I was already dressed and had decided to take her to the new little Italian restaurant in town. I got up and slipped on my riding jacket. "I'll see you guys later."

I wanted to stop and get flowers for my girl before I picked her up. I mounted my bike and headed to Coming up Roses, the only flower shop in our small town. I pulled up in front of the shop and went inside. Iris, the owner, was fixing a bouquet at her table near the back. I looked around and spotted a lovely bouquet of daisies and roses mixed. I liked those best so I picked up a bunch and took them over to pay for them.

"Hey Fang, how is it going?" Iris asked. She had gone to school with Katherine. They weren't close but they had hung out some so I knew her. She was a nice girl, just not my type.

"Doing good Iris, how are you?" I asked politely as I paid for the flowers. She handed me my change and then a box for the flowers to keep them safe.

"I'm doing fine, work is busy so I can't complain. You are dating someone?" she asked curiously. I just smiled at her.

"Yes, these are for Cara Daniels." I told her as I headed for the door. I was ready to see my girl.

I secured the box and rode to her apartment. I knocked on the door and she answered wearing a pair of fitted jeans and a long sleeve shirt with one shoulder bare. It was cute, she also had on some boots and had a jacket in her hand.

"You look beautiful, these are for you." I opened the box and handed her the flowers." Her eyes lit up and she looked up at me smiling.

"Thank you, they are so lovely. I'll put them in water really quickly before we go. Come on in." She turned and went to find a vase. I walked behind her and took the vase down off the top of the fridge for her. I got a whiff of her perfume, and she smelled like oranges. So fresh and delicious. "Thanks." She murmured as she filled the vase with water and then arranged the flowers. Putting them on her counter.

4

C^{ara}

" Hey baby, you look beautiful. Would you like to go for a ride?" he asked me as I saw the extra helmet. Biting my lip, I looked at him and then again at the bike.

"Hell yeah!" I said as I turned to lock my door and put my cross-body purse on. He helped me slide my jacket on and then he put the helmet on me.

"Have you ridden a motorcycle before?" he asked me as we approached his bike. I shook my head and he winked at me. "Just climb on behind me. Put your feet on these pedals away from pipes. Wrap your arms around my waist tight, if I lean you lean. Got it?"

"Got it." I said as I watched him mount his bike and offer me a hand so I could swing a leg over. As I settled into the seat I got as close as I could and wrapped my arms around his waist. He put one of his hands over both of mine and told me to hold on tight. Then he took off. Feeling the powerful engine under me rumbling and the heat from Fang's body had me so turned on it my panties were soaked. We rode along the city streets and then into town before he pulled into the parking lot of a local Italian place I had wanted to try. When he parked, he offered his hand to steady me as I climbed off his bike. "Oh my God, that was amazing."

"I'm glad you liked it. I'll take you for a ride anytime." He told me as he took off my helmet and attached it to his bike. I flipped my hair and then ran my fingers through it. "You look beautiful."

"Thank you." I took his offered arm and walked into the restaurant with him. The hostess looked him over like he was on the menu, and I cleared my throat shooting daggers at her.

"We have a reservation. Watson party of two." He told her as he put his arm around my waist. The hostess took a couple of menus, and we followed her to a table in the middle of the room. "We would actually like that booth over in the corner."

"Of course, I'm sorry." The flustered hostess headed to the booth near the back. I slid into the booth and Fang sat down beside me. "Your server will be right with you." I watched her walk away looking annoyed. I did a happy dance in my head. He put his arm behind me.

"You're not going to look at the menu?" I was surprised. He shook his head.

"I know what I want. I order takeout from here at least once a week." Fang said as he jerked his head toward the waiter to get his attention. The young man made his way over with a basket of fresh bread and butter as well as a couple of glasses of water.

"What can I get for you this evening?" he asked us, smiling at me. Fang growled under his breath, and I looked at him. "Would you care for an appetizer?"

"Yes, would you bring us an order of the fried ravioli and mozzarella wedges." Fang asked. "Then give the lady a minute to look over the menu. Cara, would you like a glass of wine?"

"Yes, I'd like a glass of your house Moscato please." I said as I felt Fang's hand gently rubbing my shoulder. "I would like the chicken alfredo for my entrée."

"I'll have a beer and I want spaghetti and meatballs." Fang told the waiter. "Have you eaten here before?"

"No, but that's my favorite Italian dish and I never eat out except for breakfast once a week with Sophie at the diner." I was a little embarrassed to admit that. "I'm usually working. Between the clinic and the shelter, I don't get a lot of down time."

"You don't have enough help?" He sounded genuinely interested.

"I have a couple of employees and some volunteers. I just don't have the funds right now to hire anyone else. We try to have fundraisers when we can, and I offer discounts on vaccinations when someone adopts from the shelter." I looked at him and he was completely focused on me. I wasn't used to being the center of anyone's attention, let alone a handsome, virile man. It made my stomach flutter.

5

Fang

    She was so animated when she spoke about her shelter and vet clinic. I could tell she truly loved animals. I had noticed when I went by yesterday that she really needed a larger building but that she had made the most of the space. She had an office the size of a walk-in closet and her two exam rooms were about the size of a large bathroom. All the rest of the space was dedicated to the animals that were sheltered there. She had a small room where people could get to know the dog or cat they wanted to adopt. A supply room full of food, treats and things they may need. The exam rooms had locked cabinets for the medicines. She had twenty-four kennels for the dogs and then a large room for the cats that had separate cages.

"You really love working with them, don't you?" I said as her eyes lit up. "I bet if you could you'd have more."

"Oh yes, I'd love to be able to help more. Unfortunately, I don't have the space or the staff for anymore. I hope to expand at some point." She was going to say something else when the waiter came by with our drinks and the appetizers. I heard her stomach rumble. She blushed.

"Did you eat lunch today?" I was pretty sure I knew the answer already, but she wrinkled her nose and shook her head. "Unacceptable, you need to eat."

"It's not like I'm going to blow away. It won't hurt me to miss a couple of meals." She mumbled as she stared at the food on the table. I took a small plate and put some of the ravioli and fried cheese on it along with some of the marinara sauce. I picked up a piece of the ravioli and blew on it, then dipped it in the sauce and held it to her mouth.

"Try this." I said as she took a bite and closed her eyes. "Good isn't it. I don't want to hear you talk badly about yourself. You are beautiful just the way you are." She moaned at the taste and my cock jerked in my pants. I shift a little trying to get some relief. She licked her lips and I groaned. She looked at me and smiled.

I watched her pick up one of the cheese wedges and dip it into the marinara and offer it to me. I leaned over and took a bite. She started to wipe the sauce off her fingers when I took her hand and put her finger in my mouth to suck off the sauce. Cara gasped and her eyes widened. I noticed her squirming in her seat and winked at her.

"Eat, our entrée's will be out soon." I told her as she put the rest of the cheese wedge into her mouth. They used fresh mozzarella, and it was delicious. All of their ingredients were homemade. She sipped her wine and then asked about the club.

"So, I know a little about the Rippers from Sophie. We have been friends for years. I was there for their wedding and met most of the guys and their old ladies. It wasn't at all what I expected." She said, taking a bigger sip of her wine. "How long have you been a member?"

"Well, I was raised there. My father was a patched member. I got patched around the age of twenty. I had to pledge just like anyone else. So, I have been a member for the last eighteen years." I knew she was only in her late twenties, and I wondered what she would think about the almost ten-year age difference.

"So, you have been around motorcycles and bikers your whole life." She said as she ate another ravioli. "I always had the idea that bikers were rough and mean but I know that the Rippers are well thought of in town and that you really are a big family."

"There are clubs like that. We had issues with one many years ago. We thought they were all gone then a few of their members popped up and had kidnapped some women. We got them free but not before one of them was assaulted." She looked up at me and her face paled. "I don't want you to fear all bikers and I'm not saying we are the only good club. I just want you to be careful if you come into contact with a club that you don't know anything about. It's best to steer clear until you know. Most bikers are good guys, hard working and wouldn't hurt a woman but that doesn't mean they respect them."

"The Rippers seem to be very respectful of women. At least most of them are. I've heard the stories about the parties that happen at the clubhouse." She blushed and downed the rest of her wine after she said it. I smirked. I knew what she was referring to. Our food was placed in front of us, and she declined a second glass of wine. We both just stuck to water.

"There's something you should know about those. The women that frequent those parties are what we call sweet butts or club whores. They are like badge bunnies but for bikers. They will fuck anyone with a cut. Some of the single guys do partake of what is offered, but not all. I usually don't hang around when they have them. It's never been my scene. I get my needs taken care of elsewhere. They also make sure any old ladies know that the club is off limits during those nights. Those don't happen much anymore since we have several families on the property again." I took her hand and squeezed it. "If you have any questions, you can ask me."

"That...that woman that showed up at the wedding. Was she one of those club whores?" Cara asked as she looked up at me then back down to her lap.

"She has been, but I was only with her twice and never at the clubhouse." I told her. "I told her I didn't want to see her again, that if she tried anything else that I'd fire her."

"She works at the strip club you manage?" she asked me as she put her fork down. "I'm not sure how I feel about that."

"Baby, I'm going to look for another manager so that I can go back to just working in the garage. I took the job for Hawk's old lady. Bethann used to run the club but when her sister was killed, she was left raising her nephews." I put my hand back on hers and looked her in the eyes. "I don't want anyone but you. I haven't since I first laid eyes on you."

"Okay, I believe you." She reached up and kissed my cheek. We have not kissed yet. I have been trying to be a gentleman, but I was going to kiss her before the night was over. "Is there room on your bike for us to take the rest of my food home. I'm full."

"Sure." I waved over the waiter for a carry out and our ticket. He packed her food up and I paid him. Sliding out of the booth I helped Cara out and we headed back to her place. I walked her to the door, she unlocked it and reached for my hand to pull me inside. I followed her in and heard the dogs.

"I'm going to put the food in the fridge and let them out of their crates. I'll be right back. Make yourself comfortable." She said as she put away her food and went to the other room. The dogs came out and went to get a drink from their bowl then came over for some attention. I gave them a few scratches and they went to lay down. Cara came back into the living room without her boots on and she had changed into some yoga pants. She headed to the kitchen.

"Do you want a beer or some water?" she asked me as she fixed herself some ice water.

"Water is fine. Do you want to watch a movie?" I asked her as she came to sit down beside me. She nodded and handed me the remote. I turned on one of the Star Trek series that was on, and she curled up beside me. I played with her hair some as she ran her hand up and down my chest. I was hard again and getting very uncomfortable in these jeans. She smelled so good. I looked down to find her looking at me or rather my lips and then she glanced up at me. I put my hand in her hair and pulled her to me pressing my lips to hers. She crawled into my lap straddling me and wrapped her arms around my neck. I felt her rock against my cock and groaned at how wet she was through her clothes. My girl was turned on.

I slid my tongue into her mouth, and we took turns tasting each other then I pressed kisses down her neck and sucked some of her skin in leaving little marks along her collarbone. She shivered and I pulled back to look at her. What a beautiful sight she was. Eyes glazed with passion, face flushed and my mark on her neck.

"If you want to stop, you tell me." I said as I looked at her. She sat back on my lap and pulled her sweatshirt over her head. She had no bra on. "Well okay then." I slid my hands down her back and under her thighs before standing up holding her to me. She wrapped her legs around my waist, and I carried her to the bedroom. Laying her down on her bed I pulled her leggings down to find she had also removed her panties. She started to cover herself and I shook my head.

"You can turn off the light if you want to." She whispered with her eyes closed. I stared at her for a minute. I knew women had crazy ideas about what they thought a man found beautiful. She was fuller figured with nice large breasts, a soft, round tummy and a plump pussy. I thought she was beautiful.

"Why the hell would I want to do that?" I asked her while enjoying the view. "I want to see every inch of you. I want to see your body flushed with desire and your legs tremble when I make you come. I would not change a single thing about you."

"Oh, I want to see you too." Cara said as she bit her lip and scanned my body. I pulled my shirt over my head and unbuttoned my jeans, kicking them off. I left my boxers on because I wanted to take my time.

"Scoot back against the headboard. Bend your knees and spread your legs." I told her as I climbed between her legs and put one of her ankles on my shoulder. I started to kiss up the inside of her leg to her thigh not quite to her core then did the same with the other one. I glanced up at her and she was panting, her eyes wide watching me. I winked at her and went for her plump lips. Licking and sucking her labia into my mouth one side at a time. Running my tongue through her slit up to her clit and back down. I had to put a hand on her stomach because she was writhing. She tasted so sweet I could eat her all day. I continued to suck her clit and reach up to gently twist and pinch her nipples. She moaned my name, and I slid a finger inside her. Damn, she was so tight. I wanted to be inside her, but I was going to make her come first. I added another finger and scissored them a little to loosen her up. I felt her tightening and I thrust my fingers in and out while sucking her clit and flicking it with the tip of my tongue. When I gave it a little nip she went off like a rocket. I felt her clenching around my fingers and her honey gushing all over my hand. I pulled my fingers out of her and watched her face as I sucked my fingers clean.

Her eyes were so wide, and her beautiful face was flushed. I reached down to get a condom from my pants pocket. Sliding it on, I lined myself up at her entrance and pushed in slowly. I was thicker than long, and it took some adjusting. I slid back and pushed in again until I was fully sheathed by her. She had broken into a sweat across her brow and upper lip. Her eyes were rolling, and she was panting. I ran my hand up and down her body while the other held her leg over my shoulder.

"Oh God, Fang please you have to move." She begged as she tried to move her hips.

"Jimmy, call me Jimmy when I'm buried inside your body." I told her. I wanted to hear my given name on her lips, not my road name.

"Fuck me Jimmy, I need you to fuck me hard." she demanded as she looked in my eyes. So, I took her at her word, pushed her thighs back and gave her what she wanted. I could tell she was close again.

"Play with your clit, I want to feel you come all over my cock." I was getting close, but I wanted her to come again. She reached down and started rubbing circles on her clit and her hand got faster until she cried out back arched up and she was milking every bit of come from me. I yelled her name as I spent myself inside of the condom. I gently lowered her legs, pulled out of her and went to dispose of the condom. I walked back into the bedroom and lay beside her pulling her close to me.

Chapter 6

6

*C**ara*

    I watched him come back into the bedroom and lay beside me. When he pulled me close, I fit perfectly. That was the best sex of my life. I was not a virgin. I mean I'm twenty-nine years old. I just had not found someone that rocked my world like that. Hell, I was lucky if the guy even attempted to touch my clit, never mind set up camp and feast. I was in a post-coital glow and felt like a limp noodle.

"Baby, are you okay?" He sounded concerned as he looked at me. "I didn't hurt you, did I?"

"No, that was amazing. I'm just all spent and feeling good." I giggled and hid my face against his chest. He chuckled and squeezed me tighter.

"That's a relief because I'm hoping we can do that a lot more." He tilted my chin and kissed me. I loved his kisses; I could make out with him for hours. When he pulled back, he kissed my nose and smiled.

"I need to go use the bathroom; will you stay?" I asked him, suddenly feeling insecure.

"I'd like nothing better than to sleep with you in my arms. I'm not going anywhere." He watched me walk across the room. I went into the bathroom, did what I needed to and then turned out the light to go get back in bed. I left the bathroom night light on, and the door cracked, turning off the bedroom light. I climbed back into bed, and he immediately pulled me back against his chest. I've never slept being spooned before, but I felt so warm and safe.

"Oh damn, I need to let Spock and Kirk outside before we go to sleep." I mumbled. I started to get up, but Fang stopped me.

"Your back yard is fenced in, right? I'll let them out, you stay warm." He kissed me on the cheek and threw on his boxers to go let the boys outside. I yawned and felt myself starting to fall asleep when he got back in the bed and the pups jumped up to sleep near my feet in their spot. "Night baby girl."

I woke up the next morning to my alarm going off. I was so warm and cozy I wanted to hit snooze. Of course, running an animal shelter meant I couldn't do that. I sat up and realized Fang was still in bed beside me. I took a minute to admire his chest. He worked out and stayed in shape. He was nicely built, not too bulky but defined with a sexy amount of chest hair that made me want to follow his treasure trail. Unfortunately, I didn't have time this morning. I got up and went to jump in the shower to wake up. I had to be at work in thirty minutes. I took a fast shower, dried myself off and pulled my hair into a ponytail. Slipped on some jeans and a long sleeve thin t-shirt with my logo on it and headed back into my bedroom to see Fang sitting on the side of the bed.

"Hey, sorry I didn't think about me having to get up so early. You're welcome to hang out here, sleep a little longer. I have to be at work soon to take care of the animals and I have some appointments today." I told him as I slipped on my socks and shoes. He kissed me on the head and went to the bathroom. Came back out a few minutes later and got dressed.

"I'll leave with you. I can run home, shower and change clothes then go get us both some breakfast and drop it off. I have some errands to run today." He suggested as he slipped his boots on.

"I'd like that, I have my coffee pot on a timer so let's grab a cup to go. I have to have some to function." I said as he came up behind me and kissed my neck. "Do you like anything in your coffee?"

"Black is fine, baby." He said as he took the creamer out for mine. I fixed them both and we headed out the door. "I'll see you in about an hour."

We walked out together, and he kissed me again before opening my car door and then closing it. It sounded like it was going to be a wonderful day. I cranked up my radio and jammed out while sipping on my coffee on my way to work. Spock and Kirk were in the back seat looking out the window. They both loved to ride. When I pulled up, I let them in the side entrance to the gated play area so they could take care of business. Then unlocked the front door to go inside. I had a few hours before my first appointment of the day, so I went about feeding the animals and letting them out a few at a time while I started cleaning their kennels. I heard Corinne, one of my volunteers, coming down the hall. I knew it was her because she was on the phone.

"Hey Cara, I can finish with the kennels for you. I think you have a visitor in the front." She smiled as I jumped up and headed to my office.

"I'm so sorry, I totally forgot you were coming back. I got busy." I said blushing as he winked at me. "That smells so good."

"It's okay, I just want to make sure you eat before you get too swamped. I also got you a sandwich for later." He put the other bag in my small fridge and then sat down in front of my desk. Pulling out our breakfast. I knew which coffee was mine because I could smell the yummy creamer. "What time do you finish today?"

I was chewing a bite and glanced at my day planner to see what was on my schedule. I took a sip of my coffee and put it down.

"I have about five vaccination appointments and a couple of people wanting to have their animals neutered. I have a volunteer today so I'll have help in the shelter and my assistant will be here in the next thirty minutes. I think I should be done by six." I told him as I took another bite.

"Would you be okay with me bringing dinner over tonight and spending time with you before work?" he asked me. I put my food down and felt a little queasy about him going to work at the strip club tonight. I hated that he would be surrounded by a bunch of almost naked beautiful women. "Baby, I already told you. I don't want any of them. I just want you. I'm also interviewing a couple of guys to take over as manager, so I don't have to be there anymore."

"I know and I'm sorry that it makes me uncomfortable." I grumbled looking down at my hands. He came over and picked me up, putting me on his lap.

"You are entitled to your feelings and after the way Brandi behaved, I understand. Just bear with me on this a little longer." He said as he rubbed my back. "We can have dinner; watch a movie and I can tuck you in before I go to work tonight."

"I'd like that. How about Chinese?" I suggested. I had not had that in a long time. "I'm not picky as long as it's not too spicy."

"Chinese it is. I'll see you at about six-thirty." He kissed me and then let me up. "I'll see you later, baby. Have a good day."

I finished my breakfast and my coffee then headed to the clinic to prepare for my first appointment. Tommy, my assistant, walked in and started to prepare for each appointment. He would set up trays for each one with the animal's name on it and it made things go much faster. We were slammed for most of the day. When we finished with our clinic appointments, I let Tommy leave and Corinne had left an hour ago. It was almost four and I had to make sure the animals had food and water. Corinne had taken them and played with them between cleaning the kennels, so they had some interaction and affection. We were hoping for a big turnout on our adoption day. I was sweeping when I smelled smoke. I looked around trying to figure out where it was coming from. I had some straw for when we had hamsters or mice brought in. I kept it in a room near the office. I started to walk back that way and it got stronger and I saw smoke coming from that room. I immediately opened my office to let my dogs out and snagged my purse with my phone in it. I ran to the kennels and Spock and Kirk followed me. We started to open the kennels to let the animals out into the yard. The fire was spreading, and I dialed nine one-one to report the emergency. I barely got the name out when the smoke was surrounding me. I felt the heat from the fire, and I couldn't breathe. I made it near the back door thinking I was never going to see Fang again and then nothing.

7

F^{ang}

I had left the Shelter in a great mood. I had some errands to run. I needed to go to the club and do the payroll as well as a deposit. I also wanted to confirm the interviews for later. The sooner I could hire and train my replacement the better. I wanted to be on the same schedule as Cara so we could be together more. I pulled up to the club and saw Axle's bike parked out front. He normally didn't frequent the club but especially not during the day.

I walked into the main bar area and saw him sitting there with a beer in his hand. He looked like he had been at it for a while. The Rippers owned Trixie's so it's not like it was a big deal, except that Axle didn't drink often. I tried to think of what could have set him off, but I was drawing a blank.

"Hey Prez. Everything okay?" I asked as I reached the bar and tossed his empties and started a pot of coffee. He looked up at me and then back down at his wallet. I glanced over and noticed it was a picture of Bear's sister. Valkyrie had been taken by a rival gang, brutally raped and beaten then left for dead. Axle had been in love with her. It dawned on me that it was the anniversary of her death.

"Just thinking about Kelly and what she would be doing if she was still with us." He slurred as he stared blankly at the picture, likely remembering things. "I kind of like the waitress at the Diner, but I feel like I'd be cheating on Kelly and that it's wrong."

"You know Kelly would want you to move on and be happy. Would you have wanted her to mourn you this long and never be happy or take a chance again?" I took the beer he had in front of him and poured it down the drain. I handed him a bottle of water. "Drink this and go crash in the breakroom. I'll be in my office doing payroll."

Axle scowled at me, downed the water and headed to the back. He knew he wasn't in any shape to ride at the moment, and I wasn't about to let him keep drinking. I watched him until he closed the door. Axle was a handsome bastard, but he could be mean as a snake when he was crossed. Luckily, I had known him his whole life, so he knew not to start any shit with me. I poured myself a large cup of coffee and headed to my office.

I had finished up payroll and was about to call to confirm interviews when my phone rang. I saw Remy's name on the caller ID.

"This is Fang?" I answered in a clipped tone. I was still irritated about his brother's stunt at the wedding.

"Man, you need to get over to Liberty Memorial now. There was a fire at the shelter, and I found the little vet passed out by the back door with smoke inhalation animals running around everywhere. I called some volunteers to get crates for them and round them up. The ambulance took Dr. Daniels to the emergency room, she is going to need oxygen and to be monitored for a few days. Two of the dogs had collars with her name and number on them. I had Blade come get them and take them to the clubhouse." Remy said calmly.

"FUCK! Thanks for calling me. I'm heading there now." I said as I left and headed to the hospital. I passed the shelter on the way, and it was in really bad shape. She was going to be crushed. I didn't stop to assess the damage, but I would be checking with Remy and Luke later to find out what started it. She was very careful, and I couldn't imagine what could accidentally start a fire there. I was walking into the emergency room when I saw my sister coming over to me.

"Where is she? How is she?" I demanded looking at Katie. She put her hand on my arm and led me over to the chairs.

"They are working on her now. They are having to insert a tube down her throat to keep her airway open. She will be on oxygen until she regains consciousness. We will monitor her closely. Remy got her here very quickly so she should make a full recovery, but she will need to be under observation for the next 24-48 hours. She had a little bump on her head, likely from where she fell. I'll let you know as soon as I have more information." Katherine looked at me and hugged me. "Stay here and I'll let you know when you can see her. I called Gears and he will tell Sophie."

"I'm not going anywhere until I see her." My sister nodded and went back to work. I was sitting there with my head in my hands when Sophie came in with Gears arm around her.

"Where is she?" Sophie asked, crying. "Where are her dogs?"

"Spock and Kirk were taken to the clubhouse. Fury will make sure they get taken care of and settled. The firefighters called volunteers to get the rest of the animals in carriers and moved them somewhere temporarily. I can't think about that until I know she's okay." I said as I glanced at my brother's girl. I knew that she and Cara were super close. "I'm sure she will be fine. She is strong and Remy found her quickly."

"We need to figure out how to help her. I don't know that she has much insurance. I think it mostly covered the clinical side. She opened the shelter a few years ago when she found out the other one was a kill shelter." Sophie said. "She can barely afford her apartment because everything she makes aside from her basics goes to that shelter and her clinic."

We were all sitting around the waiting room hoping for some news on Cara's condition when I saw Doc and Katherine walk up. I jumped up out of my chair and walked over to my sister and my friend.

"Fang, she is stable, but she hasn't woken up yet. You can go sit with her and talk to her." Doc said as he looked around and saw Gears with Sophie laying across his lap.

"Any idea why she hasn't woken up yet?" I asked him, my stomach was tight, and my heart hurt thinking about the fact that I could have lost her today.

"She works too much. Her body is just taking this time to rest. Go sit with her and just page a nurse if she wakes up. I'll be in to check on her later." Doc said as he headed back to the trauma room.

"Gears, why don't you take Sophie home and I'll call you when Cara wakes up." I suggested. "I also need you to see if Hawk can do the interviews for me tonight. I'm not leaving."

"Sure, I'll wake her in a few minutes and get her home. Let us know if you need anything. We will go get the dogs and look after them at our place. They know Sophie so they will do better with us. I'll also see what I can find out about the other animals that have been displaced."

"Thanks, I want to do what I can to help. I'm waiting to hear from Remy and Luke about what caused the fire and what is left of her building. Call me later." I turned and walked down the hall to where Katherine said her room was. She looked so pale lying in the hospital bed. Her hair was a dirty mess, and she had a bruise on the side of her face where she fell. I picked up a chair and put it beside the bed and sat down. Placing her hand in mine, I stroked her hand and prayed she would wake up soon. I wish I had asked her out sooner. She meant so much to me already.

"Baby, I need you to wake up. I need to see those pretty brown eyes." I talked softly to her. Gently running his other hand through her hair. She still didn't move. I brought her hand to my lips and held it. I felt her move a little and looked up to see her trying to open her eyes. She started trying to talk. "Baby be calm, I'll get the doctor to come take out the tube. I pushed the call button for a nurse. A few minutes later I saw Doc come into the room. Cara looked panicked.

"Hey there, we were wondering when you would wake up. Hang on and I'll get that out of your throat." Doc said as he worked to remove the tubing. When he had it out, he checked her throat and her airways. "Looks much better. Your throat will be sore so try not to talk too much. Text if you can mostly. I'll get you some water and some Jello."

"My animals?" she croaked out, tears in her eyes. "Where..."

"I'm pretty sure all the animals got out. We have them in a safe location for now and your volunteers are checking on them. Spock and Kirk are with Gears and Sophie until you get out. I need you to rest. We will figure this out together." I told her. I put her cell phone in her hand. "Text, don't talk. Let your throat rest so it can heal. You had a lot of smoke inhalation."

What are we going to do with the animals? How bad is the damage?

"I don't know yet. We are waiting for the report from the fire chief. I'm going to talk to Axle about hosting an adoption day on Ripper's property this coming weekend.

I'm not sure what supplies I have left to work with for vaccinations.

Cara looked so lost and upset. I was going to take care of this as soon as I could get her back to sleep.

"Baby, I don't want you to worry about that. You text me what you need, and we will get it." I could tell she wanted to argue with me but suddenly she was holding her throat. "Are you hurting?"

She nodded her head and closed her eyes. I hit the call button, and a nurse came in. She administered some pain medicine and told us that she would likely sleep the rest of the afternoon. She texted me her list as she started to nod off. I really didn't want her to worry about any of it. I sent the group message to all the guys that I wanted to meet in an hour. Gears said he would bring Sophie up here to sit with her so she wouldn't be alone. Cara had fallen asleep not long after the nurse administered the pain meds. She told me that it was best, she would heal faster the more she rested. About fifteen minutes later, Gears and Sophie came into the room. Sophie walked over and I got up so she could sit down.

"She woke up for a few minutes, but she was hurting so the nurse gave her some pain meds and said she will likely sleep the rest of the afternoon. If she wakes before I get back let her know I'll be here later." Sophie hugged me and then sat down by her friend.

"I will, I brought some snacks and a book to read while she sleeps." Sophie looked up as Gears bent down to kiss her. "See you later."

"Later baby, I'll pick you up this evening." Gears said as we left. We met up at the clubhouse with everyone else.

Walking in I saw Axle was at the counter nursing some coffee, so I just jerked my head in his direction. He knew I wouldn't say anything about what happened earlier. We all gathered around the big table. Remy and Luke were the last to get there. They had just gotten off a shift at the fire station and had to write up the report of the Shelter fire.

"Hey so it was arson, we found a can of gasoline beside the straw she kept in the storage room. It had been poured all over it. The damage is extensive. The building will have to be torn down. It isn't safe to use." Remy said looking disgusted. "If we can help with anything let us know."

"That's actually part of why I called the meeting. She had about twenty-five animals that are now displaced. She had planned on doing an adoption day this coming weekend to help find homes for them. Now she doesn't have anywhere to do it. We have the old barn where we used to work on cars, and it's not being used. It's in good shape and since it's right by the front gate it would be easily monitored." I said looking at the guys.

"If Axle's cool with it I'm glad to help get it ready and help out." Undertaker said, scratching his beard. All the guys piped in about splitting the chores and helping out.

"Of course it's fine with me. She is your girl which makes her one of us. We take care of our own." Axle said. "Let's get a list of everything we need and assign some of the pledges to work. Then we can get the animals moved here. I'm sure Doc can help with the clinic part some, as far as getting access to medications and equipment she needs."

"Alright let's go have a look and see what needs to be done to make it functional." Axle said as we all headed over to the old barn.

8

Cara

I woke up and felt like I had been run over by a truck. My head hurt, my throat felt scratchy, and I was hearing a beeping noise. I cracked my eyes open and looked around the room to find I was in the hospital. Then I remembered the conversation I had with Fang earlier. I also remembered the fire and trying to get all my animals into the backyard. I looked over and saw Sophie with a book in her hand. Licking my lips I tried to speak but it was more like a croak. She looked up and smiled at me.

"Here, let me get you some water for your throat." She said, pouring some in a cup with a straw and bringing it to me. "Do you want me to raise your bed a bit?"

I nodded at her. She helped me drink some and then put the cup on the tray beside me. I closed my eyes and sighed. I have been having a great week so far. Things were great with Fang, and we were getting to know each other then this. I just didn't understand how it could have started. There was a light knock on the hospital room door and Detective Whittaker poked his head in.

"Hey Cara, how are you feeling?" he asked gently as he glanced over at Sophie. "Can I talk to you alone for a few minutes?"

"Sophie can stay." I said, narrowing my eyes at him. He chuckled and nodded.

"Ok, sure she can stay. I got the report on how the fire started but I'm trying to make sense of it. They found a can of gasoline in the room where it originated." He looked at me and I frowned.

"I don't keep gasoline anywhere on the premises and nothing flammable in that room at all." I told him, confused. "I don't know how that could have gotten there."

"Is there anyone who would have a grudge against you?" the detective asked. I shook my head, but Sophie put her hand on my leg.

"Cara was Fang's date to his sister's wedding. One of the strippers at the dance club he works at didn't take it very well. She was pretty pissed." Sophie said, looking at me.

"You really think she would do something like that because we were on a date?" I was horrified. "I put everything I have into that clinic and the shelter. I barely have enough insurance to cover the clinic supplies but the building I got on a foreclosure deal, or I never could have afforded it."

"I'm terribly sorry about that, Ms. Daniels. If you think of anything else, please call me. I'll leave my card here on the nightstand." He left and it was just Sophie and me.

I closed my eyes as tears threatened to overtake me. What had I ever done to deserve so much bad luck? Why is it that when I was finally happy this had to happen? Sophie handed me one of her books and winked.

"You may as well read some smut with me since we have nothing else to do right now." Sophie and I both giggled. She sat back in her chair, and I raised my feet up and propped the book on my knees. She knew I was too stressed to talk about Fang at the moment. At least the book would help distract me for a while.

Katherine came in an hour later to check on me. She brought me some food and a Diet Dr. Pepper. She figured I was starving and there was no reason why I couldn't eat. She had brought me some homemade dumplings so it would be easy to swallow.

"I'm about to get off shift, but I thought you might like to see one of the pictures we got before you left the wedding." Katherine sent the photo to my phone. "For what it's worth, I have not seen Jimmy this happy in years. You're good for him."

I watched her leave as my phone pinged. I looked down and there was a snapshot of Fang looking down at me with a smile on his face and I was looking back at him. It was a great picture and I loved it.

"Well, are you going to show me?" Sophie reached for my phone, and I stuck my tongue out at her. She took it and grinned so big. "You two look so cute together. He obviously adores you. He has been grilling me for things you like for months."

"He is such a gentleman, and he is always trying to take care of me. It's really sweet. I'm just not used to it." I touched the picture on my screen and made it my screensaver. I set my phone down and started to eat my dinner. It was delicious. I finished it before I realized and was a little sad there was no more there, but I was full, so it was for the best. "That was nice of Katherine to bring me dinner."

"She's really sweet. All the guy's wives are sweet. They just kind of adopt you into the family." She said smiling as she saw a message pop on her phone. "The guys are headed back here."

"Omg, I must look horrible. Can you help me to the bathroom and brush my hair for me please?" I said panicking about him seeing me looking all pale. She shook her head.

"I'll help you to the bathroom and then I'll braid your hair so it's out of your way. If Fang hears you degrading yourself, he will have a fit." Sophie helped me by undoing my IV from the line long enough for me to go to the bathroom. When I was finished, I got back into bed, and she attached it back. She pulled a brush and a hair tie from her purse and French braided my hair gently. It felt so much better. I'd love to wash it, but I can't do that right now. We turned on the television to watch the news and they were showing footage of my building burning. It was horrific. They flashed to the aftermath and there was hardly anything left of it. I started bawling and Sophie turned the tv off.

The guys came in at that moment and Fang freaked out. He ran over to me and put his arms around me.

"What's wrong baby?" he asked as Sophie looked up at the tv and back at him. Then he realized I had seen what was left of my business. Sophie came over and gave me a hug.

"We are going to leave you two alone but just know you have people. We will help you get back on your feet." She said softly as Gears led his wife out of the room.

"What am I going to do? I sunk everything into my business. I was just starting to save a little. I have no way to pay my bills after next month. I have just enough money put aside for two months of my household bills. That's it. I don't know how much the insurance company will pay out and I'll never be able to replace that building with it." I buried my face in his chest and sobbed. He sat on the bed and pulled me into his lap rubbing my back.

"I'm too heavy to sit in your lap." I mumbled under my breath. He growled and held me tighter.

"Nonsense, you are perfect, and I love all of your curves. You will be okay. I have a suggestion. You may feel like it's too soon but I'm going to suggest it anyway." He gently put me away just enough to see my face. "I have been living in the clubhouse in one of the rooms since Katherine and Rider got married. I gave Kat the house we grew up in. I am going to have a house built on the property, but I wondered if I could stay with you and help with the bills while it's being built."

"I don't even know how I'm going to pay my half after the end of next month." I rubbed my head which was starting to hurt again.

"Have you eaten anything?" he asked me gently massaging my temples. I nodded and laid my head down on his chest. "Ok baby. Let me see about getting you something for the pain and I'll stay the night with you. Hawk is covering and doing interviews for me at Trixie's."

"Thank you." I whispered. A nurse came in and gave me something in my IV that made me sleepy. She said something to Fang about being in my bed and he responded rather gruffly but stayed where he was.

8

Fang

When I came in the girls had clearly been watching the news. I messaged Gears and asked him what they had seen. After he spoke with Sophie, I understood why she was distraught. I wanted to surprise her with the barn being equipped as a Clinic/Shelter. There was a huge loft area upstairs that we decided we could easily close in and make a three-bedroom apartment out of it for us. That way my house money could go towards the barn being fixed up for both. I wanted her to be with me and I knew it was soon but maybe if we get the business side up and running, I can have time to convince her to move in with me on the property.

I closed my eyes and we slept. I knew if Doc came in to check on her, he would wake me to give me an update. She was breathing a lot better. She still had a slight cough, but they said that was to be expected and should go away in a few days.

Doc came in around five in the morning and checked her stats. He chuckled when he saw me in bed with her. I flipped him off. She was sleeping soundly and if me holding her helps that then so be it.

"When can I take her home?" I asked him quietly. Doc sighed looking at her.

"I'd like her to stay one more night for observation. Smoke inhalation is nothing to take lightly. If she is still breathing well in the morning you can take her home." Doc said before leaving to finish his rounds. I would ask Sophie to bring her some fresh pajamas and undergarments later, so she didn't have to stay in the hospital gown. I figured she would sleep a little longer and I didn't want to wake her trying to get up, so I pulled the blanket back up over us and closed my eyes. A little while later Undertaker and Annie knocked on the door poking their head in.

"Baby, you have visitors." I whispered in her ear. She reached up and rubbed her eyes and opened them. "Can you give us like five minutes so she can go to the bathroom. These gowns leave nothing to the imagination.

"You bet; we will step into the hall just let us know when it's safe to come back in. Annie brought her a nightgown, clean panties and some fuzzy socks to keep her feet warm. I'll set the bag on this chair." Undertaker winked and then closed the door behind them.

"How would you like a quick sponge off in the bathroom and then we can get these clean clothes on you?" she blushed and nodded her head. "Ok, Doc took the IV out but said you had to stay one more night. Let's get you squared away."

I got up and then picked her up and carried her into the bathroom. I sat her down in front of the toilet and stepped outside the door for a minute. When she said she was done I went back inside with her fresh clothes and put them on the counter. I took a washcloth and got it wet, put some body wash on it and helped her clean up. Sophie had braided her hair so that was ok for now. I'd wash it for her tonight if she wanted. After I toweled her off, I helped her put on the clean clothes and get back into the bed. Then opened the door so they could come back in and visit.

"Thank you for bringing me some clean clothes to wear. I feel so much better not wearing a peek-a-boo gown." She giggled and so did Annie. I didn't like her wearing a peek-a-boo gown either. Too many chances for others to see what's mine. Annie squeezed her hand.

"Hey little lady, don't you worry about anything. We are all going to help you get opened back up. You are too good to the animals in the community for them to lose you." Undertaker said firmly as he smiled down at her. "You're with this knucklehead now so you are one of us and we take care of our own. You just focus on resting and feeling better."

I have known Undertaker all my life. He was the president of the club when I first patched in until his wife got sick. When he stepped down, he tapped Axle as his replacement and just stood in as an advisor. When Annie showed up, we started to see the guy we used to know, the one that was fun-loving and mischievous.

Their son Mattie was also a huge blessing to him. His first wife was not able to bear children, but Annie got pregnant from a one-night stand that he didn't remember and now they are expecting a second child. She was a sweetheart and she kept him feeling young. I wondered if Cara would want kids. I wasn't getting any younger.

"I'm not sure what I'm going to do. I have to find out first if the insurance is going to pay and how much they will pay. I may have to just reopen the clinic and start saving to add on another shelter." She looked so sad when she said that. I knew she loved working with animals. Truth be told, I enjoyed being around them too. I think we could start annual fundraisers and of course I have plenty of money in the bank. Maybe I could convince her to let me be her partner. The clinic would be all hers and I would run the shelter with her help and the help of volunteers.

"Baby, we will figure it out. We are also going to have the Adoption Day at the compound on Saturday. We will have a cookout with hot-dogs and hamburgers. The ladies are getting sides and desserts figured out. It will be a community wide picnic and Pet adoption. There will also be a few bouncy houses and games for the kids. We will take donations to rebuild the shelter." I told her as her eyes got wide and tears filled them.

"I have only been here one day, right? How did you organize this so quickly?" she asked me, surprised.

"We have Bethann, Lillian, Sophie, Katherine and Annie. They are all working on it along with some of the guys. We have a surprise for you when you get out of here tomorrow." I told her watching her face light up. "Speaking of that, why don't you and Annie visit for a few minutes while we talk outside."

"Okay, thank you." She whispered looking at me with those soft doe eyes of hers. She could get me to do just about anything when she looks at me like that.

Once we got outside, I turned and asked how the building was coming. I knew that we had hired a crew to come in and work as quickly as possible. We had done a lot of jobs for some very wealthy people, so we all had nice nest eggs put away. I had never had anything to spend mine on. I lived in a house that was paid for and now I am living in the clubhouse. I had very few living expenses, so all my money had been socked away earning interest. Gears made sure we were all invested in good stock options. I wanted the building finished this week. The weather was nice, and we had no problem getting the materials delivered. She was in for a huge surprise.

"Everything is coming along quickly. I feel like I'm watching an episode of that Extreme home makeover show that used to be on. It's a great set up. The plans are amazing. The upstairs living space is sound proofed so that you don't hear the animals and they don't hear you. There looks to be enough kennels to hold forty animals. Gears set up a webpage with a donation link. It is currently listed as Liberty Animal Rescue. He said there is a nice chunk of money already donated. We set up an account that we will put her on as soon as she is able to go to the bank with me. There is a separate space for the clinic with four exam rooms, a storage unit and a small office space for her. There is a dog run attached to the back side where the shelter is and two playrooms for people to spend time with an animal to see if they are a good fit. It is coming together nicely. We reached out to a vet in the next county to find out what all we needed to stock the clinic with. He was very helpful. If she freaks out, tell her that we own the business and want her to run it." He scratched his beard and turned to walk back to the room. I followed him grinning like an idiot.

We walked back into the room, and they were looking at pictures on Annie's phone. Cara looked up and smiled at me. She seemed to be in better spirits. Annie gave her a hug and left with her old man. I went and sat down in the chair by her bed.

"Did you have a nice visit?" I looked around for a menu. "What do you want to eat?"

"I'd love some oatmeal with bananas and walnuts. It just sounds good today." She looked like she could sleep some more.

"I'll call in an order to the Diner. Why don't you close your eyes and rest until I get back with it?" I suggested as her eyelids drooped. I heard her mumble okay and she was asleep again. I kissed her on the forehead and went to get her food.

Walking into the Diner I decided to order a sandwich for her lunch as well. I placed our food orders and sat at the counter to wait. Dani, our regular waitress, put a cup of coffee in front of me and fixed a mocha latte for Cara. I had been buying them for her for the last two months. I just smiled and put a fifty-dollar bill on the counter.

"No change, thanks for taking care of us." I told her. She smiled and shook her head at me as she went on to wait on someone else. I got our food order and as I was leaving, I noticed Brandi sitting in the back watching me. Ugh, seriously. I told her I wasn't interested. I walked out and put the food in my truck. I knew I would be bringing Cara home tomorrow, so I didn't want to bring my bike. Her car was a total loss due to being too close to the building. I would have to break that to her later. She had not thought to ask, and I figured she had enough bad news.

10

Cara

I woke up to Fang coming back to my room with food. My stomach rumbled and I blushed. He just laughed and put one bag on the window seal and the other he put on my tray. I had my favorite coffee and the oatmeal I had asked for. I started on it as soon as he handed me the spoon. I fell asleep before dinner last night, so I had not eaten since lunch yesterday. He got himself one of the breakfast sandwiches. We ate in silence, and it was nice. I loved that we could spend time together and didn't have to talk. When I finished my breakfast, I started to get up.

"Woah, where are you going?" Fang asked me as he took my arm to help me up.

"I just have to use the bathroom; I can do it myself." I grumbled. I felt bad for snapping at him, but I was going crazy in this room, and I missed my dogs. He raised an eyebrow at me, and my shoulders sagged. I looked up at his handsome face and put my arms around him. "I'm sorry, I'm bored and cranky. I didn't mean to snap at you. Let me go to the bathroom. I'll be right out. I promise to call out if I feel weird."

"Okay baby. I understand. You are not used to being still this long." He said as he sat back down. I went and took care of my needs and then came back out. "I thought tomorrow we could swing by your insurance office, and you can go ahead and see what you need to fill out or sign, after that I'd like to take you somewhere to show you the surprise I mentioned. I hope you like it."

"I'm sure I'll love whatever it is. I'm just so ready for some sunshine on my face." I said looking out the window. "I hate that we didn't get to have our other date last night. You were sweet to stay here with me in this uncomfortable hospital bed."

"I wouldn't have wanted to be anywhere else. I actually got some sleep because you were safe in my arms. I think if I had tried to sleep at the clubhouse I would have had nightmares about you in the building." He said as he kissed me gently. "I don't want to let you out of my sight anytime soon."

"I like the sound of that. I feel like we have moved really fast but at the same time it feels right." I looked up at him wondering what he was thinking. He was grinning and I felt better.

"I'm really glad you feel that way too. I was worried that I was rushing things with us. The thing is, I have liked you for quite some time. I just wasn't sure you would want to go out with someone almost ten years older than you." He said, sounding a bit unsure of himself. "Now I don't want to let you get away."

"I'm not going anywhere. I didn't think you would want to deal with my busy schedule. Most guys don't understand why I'm always at the shelter and why I can't just leave the animals to someone else to deal with." I know my voice gave away my frustration with those thoughts. I love animals, more than most people.

"I think it's sweet that you care so much. They are lucky to have you. I hope that you will let me help. I really enjoyed seeing you work with them, and I have always liked animals." Fang sat on the bed beside me and handed me the remote. "Why don't you find something for us to watch?"

We cuddled on the bed and watched some mindless show and I dozed on and off. I knew it was due to overworking myself and then the smoke inhalation. I was worried about the animals, but Fang had assured me that they were being taken care of and that Sophie was spoiling my pups. Knowing that really helped. I noticed he was texting back and forth with a few people, and I figured it was some of his brothers. I wasn't nosy by nature, I had too much going on to worry about that. I also trusted him. I had no reason not to since he has been by my side throughout this mess. I had so much to do when I got released. That's when I realized that I had not asked about my car and no one had mentioned it.

"Um, Fang?" I watched as he looked up from his phone, giving me his full attention. "Where is my car?"

He closed his eyes for a minute and then looked at me with a frown. "I'm sorry baby, it got caught in the fire. It's totaled. Remy got pictures of everything for you when he took them for the fire investigation. He sent them to your work email."

"I see. Well, I guess that is something else I'll deal with tomorrow when you take me by the insurance office." I closed my eyes and just laid there for a minute. I had my work email set up on my phone but really, I didn't want to see those pictures right now. I will look at them tomorrow when I visit the insurance office. They would probably cancel my policy after this. One more thing to think about. "I don't feel very good, I think I'm going to try to sleep some more."

"Are you feeling sick or achy, should I get Doc?" he asked me, concerned.

"No, just queasy from all the bad news." I said as I closed my eyes. I curled on my side facing away from him so he wouldn't see the tears rolling down my face. He curled up behind me and just ran his fingers through my hair in a soothing manner. It felt good and soon I was asleep.

The next morning Doc came in and signed my release papers. Fang was going to stay at my place with me. We got my stuff together and left the hospital. Sophie had dropped off some fresh clothes for me to wear home and a pair of shoes since mine were ruined. He was taking me by the insurance company first so we could get that over with and then he wanted to show me my surprise. He was as giddy as a kid on Christmas.

Walking into the insurance office I was met by my agent who had already received a call from the Fire Chief and the police department. He had my claims all ready for me to sign and disperse. I was shocked that it was so easy. He said due to it being arson and the police clearing me of any wrongdoing they wanted to make sure I had what I needed to get things back up and running. I looked up at Fang in shock. He shrugged his shoulders. I knew they probably had something to do with this being facilitated so quickly but I decided to just shut up and be grateful.

"So, are you ready for your surprise?" he asked me as we walked back to the truck.

"Absolutely. I can't wait to see what has you so excited." I laughed at his enthusiasm. Whatever it was had to be epic because he was beyond excited to show me. We headed to the compound and as we approached the gate, I noticed the barn had been renovated. It had a sign on the front that read 'Liberty Clinic and Animal Rescue'. It was massive, we pulled inside the gates, and he parked out in front of it.

"Okay, before you get mad or defensive, let me explain." Fang said as he opened my door for me. "I grew up here, I always knew I would be a member. I did a brief stint in the military and then had to come home to take care of my sister when my father passed. I never got a chance to really figure out what I wanted to do. I have plenty of money from jobs we have done and did not have many expenses. I love animals just like you do. I thought we could run this together. I can work more on the shelter side, and you run the clinic. What do you think?"

He looked so nervous. I looked at the building and thought that it would be selfish of me to turn him down. The animals needed this and so did I. He wanted this as well.

"I love that idea. So, you would not be working at the strip club anymore?" I asked, looking up at him. He smiled at me and picked me up.

"Nope, I'll be working with my girl." He said smiling. "There is a little more to the surprise, but it won't be done until tomorrow, so this is all you get for today. I just wanted you to see it so you would be able to sleep well tonight. Let's go get your babies and head home. I can fix us some dinner and we can watch movies."

"Sounds good. I miss the little monsters. I hope they were good for Gears and Soph." I waited for him to open my door and we drove the short distance to their place to pick up my pups. Sophie met us at the door with them and she was jumping on her heels excitedly.

"What did you think, isn't it awesome?" she asked me with a huge grin on her face. I smiled and hugged her.

"I love it. I can't wait to see the inside. He won't let me see until it's finished." I pouted as I looked up at my guy. He winked and took the leashes from her.

"I want to take her home, so she can take a shower and have some dinner. Thanks for everything Sophie. We will see you later." Fang said as he helped me into the car and settled the dogs in the backseat. He drove us back to my place. When we pulled up, he parked in front and helped me out of the car then took the pups and we went inside. "Let me feed them and then we will get you a shower and I'll wash your hair for you."

"That sounds like heaven." I said as I watched him take the leashes off and put them up then get their food. Spock and Kirk both loved Fang already. We had been flirting and talking for a few months now. He has been bringing me food and coffee and checking on me to make sure I'm eating. Bringing me flowers and little treats. I am so head over heels in love with this man already. It doesn't matter that it hasn't been very long. I know my heart and he has shown me that I can trust him.

"I ordered our dinner so let's get you in the shower and in some clean comfy clothes before it gets here." Fang said as he offered his hand to help me up off the couch. He led me into the bathroom and started to remove my clothes, dropping them in the hamper. Turning on the shower, he checked the temperature and then stripped off his own clothes.

"Just relax and let me take care of you baby." He murmured as I wet my hair down and he took the shampoo then massaged some through my hair. Turning me to rinse it out then applying conditioner. I handed him the loofah and he squirted some body wash on it and started to wash my body. It felt amazing. Whenever he touched me, I got turned on. If I had on panties they would be soaked through right now. He knelt down and cleaned my feet and legs then back up to my pussy. He did a cursory clean there and my back hole then rinsed me off. "I'd love to do more but our dinner will be here soon. Hop out while I finish and put on something comfortable." He gave me a kiss on the forehead and swatted my behind. I squealed and laughed.

I dried myself off and used the blow dryer on my hair just to take most of the moisture out of it. Then I put on some joggers and a long shirt. He came out of the bathroom, and I noticed a duffle bag on the floor. He pulled out some sweatpants and pulled those on. We heard the doorbell, so he went to answer it.

11

Fang

We were supposed to eat Chinese food the other night, so I ordered that. I had messaged Sophie to see what she liked to eat. Putting the food on the table I grabbed a few plates and fixed us both some ice water. I put the food in the middle of the table so she could help herself to whatever she wanted. I got plenty to share and to have leftovers.

Cara walked into the room and took a deep breath, smiling. Looking at the food on the table she skipped over and swiped a wonton, putting it in her mouth and moaning.

"Oh, that is so good. How did you know what I liked?" she asked as she saw the sesame chicken, beef and broccoli as well as the egg drop soup and crab wontons.

"I have my sources." I winked at her and held out a chair for her to sit down. "Let's eat."

She put a little bit of everything on her plate and started eating. I loved seeing her have a good appetite. I could tell she was much more relaxed since we got home. I put a notepad and a pen beside her.

"I want you to write down anything that you think you will need for the new clinic and shelter. Think big! We are going to do this right." I told her as her eyes got wider.

Looking up I realized that she had stopped eating and was staring at my chest. I saw her visibly swallow and lick her lips. Oh, my girl was feeling needy.

"See something you like baby?" I asked her as I got up and walked over to her. She nodded looking up at my face while she slipped her hands into my sweats and lowered them over my ass. I had not put on anything underneath so now she was sitting there with my cock in her face. Looking up at me through her lashes she wrapped a hand around the base and leaned in to lick the precum off the tip before sucking me into her mouth. I moaned. God this woman was a natural.

"Is your throat okay?" I asked her as I prayed, she would say yes. I didn't want her to have any pain, but I didn't want her to stop either. This felt so fucking good. She bobbed her head and licked up the shaft circling the head again. She reached around and grabbed my ass pulling me closer to where her nose touched my groin. Seeing her mouth stretched over my shaft was the sexiest thing I had ever seen. It was all she could do to get her mouth around me. I massaged her head as she bobbed, licked and sucked. "Baby, if you don't want to swallow you better back up because I'm not going to last." I grunted out. She held me to her and continued until I felt it hit and I released down her throat. She licked me clean and then sat back in her chair with a self-satisfied smile on her face. DAMN!

"That was fun." She said winking at me. The little minx. She giggled and took a drink of her water. I put the leftovers away and went to sit on the couch with her and the pups. We cuddled while watching a movie. She fell asleep with her head in my lap. Spock was laying at her feet and Kirk was on the floor by the couch. I looked around thinking this was what I wanted for the rest of my life. This sweet woman and her animals made me feel complete. Luckily the barn had been in good shape, so the bare bones were there and with the large crew we hired. They were working around the clock to finish. I could not wait to see her face when she saw everything on the inside. I eased out from under her and moved the pup so I could carry her to bed. She wrapped her arms around my neck, and I heard her mumble "I love you, Jimmy.".

I looked down at the sleepy woman in my arms. I couldn't believe how lucky I was. Placing her under the covers I kissed her on the forehead. "I love you too Cara." I shucked the sweatpants and crawled in beside her. Tomorrow was going to be a busy day. We had to move the animals to the new shelter and have her check to see if anything else was needed before Saturday's event. I also needed to get to the bottom of who set the fire in the first place. They could have killed my girl and that was not acceptable. Someone was going to pay.

The next morning, I got a call from Gears telling me to come by the clubhouse. He told me that Cara had cameras on the clinic side and that the footage was sent to the cloud, so he was able to access it. I got up, got dressed and kissed her on the cheek. She was sleeping so soundly I didn't want to wake her. I left her a note and placed it under her phone where she would see it. I would go see what he had and then come pick her up later. I slipped her keys in my pocket and locked up behind me.

Driving to the clubhouse I thought about the crazy turn this week had taken. I went from slowly courting Cara to claiming her within the week. She seemed fine with it too. She gave me a purpose other than the jobs I did with the club. I was looking forward to the next chapter of my life as long as she was a part of it. Pulling up to the gate, Gator waved me in. Fury's half brother had turned into a solid member. I parked outside the clubhouse next to my bike. Walking in I saw the guys at the table with Gears sitting in front of his laptop. They all looked pissed.

"What's up guys?" I asked as I took a seat. Gears rubbed his hand down his face, shaking his head in disgust.

"I really wish she had been having this monitored. I wouldn't even have thought to check if Sophie had not mentioned it. Apparently, she had it installed to go back and be able to check if any of the meds came up missing. She couldn't afford to have it monitored but she had it set up to upload to the cloud automatically every fifteen minutes. I pulled up the footage from the day of the fire. When Cara was alone working in her office, Brandi came in and poured gasoline over the hay in the closet and over the floor near several doors. She also put some near the clinic storage. She lit a match and took off. I would bet she poured some over Cara's car as well so it would catch."

"But how would she know there was hay or where it would be stored? It's not like they were friends or anything." I said, confused. Gears held up his hand for me to wait a minute.

"I wondered the same thing, so I started looking at the footage a few days before. Look at this." He turned the laptop so I could see it. There was Brandi with Tommy. She was making out with him, and he led her to the closet. When they finished, she stayed behind and looked around before slipping out the door. "I don't really think he is involved. I think he is just a patsy. I sent the footage to Detective Whittaker who is planning to go pick her up."

"I think we should close the strip club, hear me out. I am thinking maybe we revamp it and make it a regular club. Bar, dancing and food. No strippers. They seem to be more trouble than they are worth." I suggested. The guys all seemed to agree with me. "We can help the girls find other jobs, but I don't want any of the clingy ones staying on to wait tables. They know we are well off and they are always trying to trap one of us. I'm over this crap."

"Yeah, I agree, and we could use another fun place in town for males and females to hang out." Blade commented. "Let's revisit this after we get the Shelter up and running."

"Ok, so you are bringing Cara here in a few hours to tour the building and to check on the animals who will be here in the next hour." Fury got up. "I'm helping with transport, so I need to head out, Axle you are coming with me?"

"Yep, let's go." Axle said as they headed out. I got up too, I needed to make sure everything was ready and go get Cara. I walked outside and drove over to the building. It looked amazing. I saw Blade coming up behind me. He had his buddy's construction company do the bid, so he helped with the build out.

"Hey, you want to peek really quick before you go get your girl?" he asked. "It's a sweet set up. I think she will love it. We have a separate entrance at the back so that visitors don't have to go through the shelter to get to your door. We also have the bedrooms over the clinic with the kennels on the other side. Although it doesn't matter since it's all sound proofed. Here are the keys to both. I had four sets made to the Shelter and Clinic and just two to the living space."

"Thanks man, I really appreciate how fast all of you worked to get this done. Tell Logan there will be a nice bonus for his guys." I said accepting the keys. "I'm going to go get Cara."

12

C *ara*

    I woke up from the best night's sleep I have had in ages. I reached over and Fangs' side of the bed was cool. I reached for my phone and saw the note under it.

    Baby,

    I went to check on some things at the compound. I will pick you up in a little while to tour the new building. Make sure you eat some breakfast. See you soon.

    Love,

    Fang

    I clutched the note to my chest and sighed. With a silly grin on my face, I put the letter in my nightstand and got up to brush my teeth and get ready for the day. I could not wait to see the inside of the building. Slipping on a pair of worn jeans and a long sleeve shirt with a puppy on it, I went and fixed myself some coffee, toast and a couple of eggs. I looked at the clock and it was ten thirty. I can't remember when I slept in like this. When I finished my breakfast, I put the dishes in the dishwasher and went to put on my shoes when I heard a knock on the door. I opened it thinking it would be Fang, but it was that slut from the wedding standing at my door. She pushed me inside and I started to scream when she tased me. I felt myself hit the floor. What the hell was that thing set on? She looked around the room and then landed a kick on my side.

"You stupid cow. You just had to get in the way. I was going to be his old lady and get my hands on his money. I don't know what he sees in a fat, smelly vet. I thought I had managed to get rid of you, but the damn firefighter had to find you too quickly. At least you don't have a business anymore. I really wanted to stand there and watch it burn to the ground, but I couldn't risk being seen." Brandi said as she looked at me and spit. "I'm going to finish you off and make it look like suicide. I mean if I were you, I'd kill myself too."

As I listened to her rant I checked to see if I could move my fingers and toes. I didn't want to bring too much attention to it, I just wanted to know if I could try and defend myself. I knew Fang would be here soon. I just hoped he wasn't too late. My side hurt bad from where she kicked me with the fucking heels. I knew I needed to keep her talking to stall for time.

"How did you know where to start the fire?" I asked her in a raspy voice. I didn't try to get up because I didn't want her to tase me again.

"Oh, that was too easy. I had seen your assistant at the club a few times and decided to start flirting with him. I let him think I was actually interested in a boring vet tech. I mean seriously the guy fell for it. I showed up at the clinic and talked him into taking me to a supply closet for a bit of fun. It was perfect. He took me to a room full of hay. I had gasoline in my car so when he left, I went and got it. You were in your office with the door closed so I had no problem setting the fire and getting out." She was still bragging when I saw a flash at the window by the door. I wanted to distract her, so I started to scream. She kicked me again and I heard a crunch. My side was on fire. As she started to raise her arm, I saw Fang behind her knock the taser out of her hand and then put her hands behind her back. Detective Whittaker came in behind him cursing.

"I told you to wait for backup." He grumbled under his breath as he cuffed her and took her out of the apartment. "I'm going to radio for an ambulance on my way out."

"Damn baby, what the hell did she do to you?" Fang said as he crouched on the floor to check me over. When he started to pick me up, I screamed. He immediately stopped.

"I think she broke a rib when she kicked me the last time." I said having a hard time getting my breath. "It hurts to breathe." I said crying. He sat on the floor with my head in his lap and stroked my hair while we waited for the ambulance.

"Baby, why did you let her in?" he asked me. "I had your keys so I would not have knocked."

"I didn't realize that. I just knew you were supposed to be back soon, so I thought it was you. As soon as I opened the door, she tazed me and then kicked me. I laid on the floor and let her rant so she wouldn't kick me again. I hurt all over and I don't want to go back to the damn hospital. I just got out." I was sobbing at this point. I was hurt and angry. I had been excited for today and now I would probably be back in the hospital.

"I'll see if Doc can check you over. As long as your rib isn't puncturing a lung, he will likely just give you pain killers." He said as he stroked my hair. The EMT's arrived then and put me on a gurney to take me to the hospital for x-rays. Fang rode with me saying one of the guys could drop his truck off for him.

Doc came into the exam room and smiled at me. "We really have to stop meeting like this young lady." I started to laugh but it hurt.

"Don't make me laugh, it hurts." I said, chastising the handsome doctor. He winked at me, and Fang growled at him. I just rolled my eyes but honestly, I loved that he was possessive.

"You were lucky that it didn't puncture a lung, I'm going to give you some pain killers. You will have to rest, and I know you are not good at that, but you will heal faster if you do. You also don't want to risk a more serious injury." He said as he handed a prescription to Fang. "Why don't you go get this filled while I have Katherine come in and we will bandage the scraps on her from the heels."

"I'll be right back." He said as he kissed my forehead. "You take care of her."

"Of course." Doc winked at me again as Fang left. I knew he was just trying to get a rise out of him. "You have that man wrapped around your finger. Enjoy it."

"I will, thanks." I closed my eyes and waited for my guy to come back. At least they caught her, and she couldn't hurt me anymore. I would have to have a talk with Tommy about job etiquette. I messaged him and asked me to call me.

Fang came back to the room about thirty minutes later with my medicine and some treats. I could not believe how lucky I was to have him.

"I want you to eat this and take a pill. We will give it a chance to kick in and then I'll take you to see the new place. Doc loaned me a wheelchair. It's just for a few days." He said as he sat beside me while we ate the burgers he picked up. When I finished and I could feel the pill working I told him I was ready to go.

"Okay, Sophie found Tommy's number and Corinne's they will both be at the Adoption Day tomorrow. It starts at eleven and ends at five. They will arrive at ten so they can help set up and so you can talk to them." He helped me into the wheelchair and took me to his truck. Gently he picked me up and placed me on the seat." After he put the wheelchair in the back he got in and we were headed to the compound. I was so excited to see the inside of the building. If only I wasn't so tender from earlier.

"I hope some big woman named Bertha makes Brandi her bitch." I mumbled under my breath as I tried to get comfortable. Fang threw his head back and laughed. It was such a wonderful sound that I smiled at him.

"My girl is feeling a little bloodthirsty today." He said as he reached for my hand and linked our fingers together. "I love it."

13

Fang

When we pulled up, I got the wheelchair out and gently picked her up and placed her in it. I wheeled her to the door and Blade opened it for us.

"Are you ready baby?" I asked her as her leg was bouncing up and down. Blade laughed, noticing her leg and stood back so I could wheel her inside. We went through her clinic first. I showed her the lobby, exam rooms, her office and the storage areas.

"OMG, how did you do all of this so quickly?" she exclaimed, looking around with her mouth hanging open and eyes wide as saucers.

"Tommy put us in touch with a neighboring vet and he was a big help himself. He feels terrible about what happened." I told her as she looked around. "We got a lot of help from them. Do you like it?"

"It's wonderful. I can't wait to use it. What about the shelter?" she asked excitedly. I wheeled her through a set of double doors in the back of the clinic that connected to the shelter space. There were two rooms. One for the dogs with about twenty kennels and one for cats with twenty cages. There were two 'getting to know you' rooms as well as plenty of storage and a huge backyard area fenced in. I wheeled her through, and she saw her animals looking right at home in their new quarters. We went through the whole space so she could see everything. As we reached the end of it, she started crying.

"Is it too much, are you hurting?" I asked her, suddenly worried she had overdone it. She looked up at me, those brown eyes shining with tears and tugged my hand.

"I love you Jimmy Fang Watson. You are the best thing to ever happen to me." She said as I leaned down to kiss her.

"There's more. Put your arms around my neck." She did what I told her and I picked her up and started walking up a staircase on the side of the building. When we got to the top I kissed her again. "Open the door baby." she turned the knob, and I walked in and put her on the couch. Stay, I'll be right back to give you the tour."

I jogged down the stairs and picked up her wheelchair to take back up so I could show her around the place. The door opened to a large kitchen area with a nice size table by a window. There was a living area with a sectional couch and a television stand and plenty of throw pillows. It was very comfortable. I took her into a bedroom that was fixed up as a guest room. There was a guest bathroom between the two bedrooms. Then I showed her to the master suite, and it was beautiful. There was a king size bed near the center with bookshelves and a sitting chair with an ottoman attached near a window. The bathroom had a separate shower and soaking tub with double vanities, and it had his and her closets. It was beautiful.

"I don't understand. What is all this?" she asked me as I got down on one knee beside her. She looked very nervous but not as much as I was.

"Cara, you took my breath away from the first time I saw you. I have been courting you for months. I know we have only had a few official dates, but I feel like you know me well enough now to know that I don't do casual dating. I want to spend my life with you. I want to work alongside you and share in all the joys and trials that life gives us. I don't expect you to marry me this week, but I would like it if you would agree to it in the future and I'd like you to move into this place with me. I had this built for us." I bared my soul to her as she caught her breath and leaned in to kiss me.

"I never thought I would find someone that loved me for me. Someone that I enjoy being with and that makes me feel whole. You are all of that. I have never had someone who wanted to take care of me. My parents weren't bad, but they were wrapped up in their own careers and too busy for me most of the time. My brothers are all much older and joined the service moving away. It's just been me for a long time. So yes, I'd love to eventually marry you and I want to live here with you and work with you." she said with emotion choking her up. "I love you so much."

"Baby, I love you too. Tomorrow is going to be awesome." I said kissing her. "Can I pack your stuff and move you in?"

"My apartment was furnished so I really don't have a lot of stuff. It wouldn't take long to pack it. How about Sunday afternoon we go over and I'll let you do it." She suggested. as I put her on the bed. "What are you doing?"

"Well, we won't be able to have sex for the next six weeks, but we can at least take a nap and cuddle." I lay down beside her and we fell asleep. She was lying on the side that wasn't hurt and I was behind her with my hand resting on her hip. I could totally get used to this.

When she woke up, I started to kiss her and she covered her mouth and wrinkled her nose.

"I need to brush my teeth and get something to drink." She said frustrated that she couldn't do much for herself at the moment. Doc said after a few days she would be able to get around better. She just couldn't do anything too strenuous. I helped her to the bathroom and then carried her to the living room.

14

C^{ara} "Sophie wanted to come hang out for a bit after work. I thought while she was here, I would go get some things done for tomorrow." Fang brought me a big, insulated cup of ice water, a sandwich with chips and handed me the remote. "I'll be back in a couple of hours, and we can decide on dinner."

Fang left to get things done and I was sitting on the couch contemplating finding a movie to watch or a series on Netflix. I enjoyed mindless television time occasionally. I just didn't get to do that very often. Thinking about how the past week had gone it felt like it had been a month instead of a week. All the drama, the fire, the crazy woman attacking her in her own home. She was glad she wouldn't have to ever sleep there again. Looking around at this place she marveled at the turn her life had taken. Her parents had not been crazy about her becoming a vet instead of a surgeon but since it was a medical field they paid for her education and when she graduated, she got her little trust fund. It had not been a lot but enough for her to start her practice.

She thought back to her friendship with Sophie. She had always been there for her and was more like a sister to her. She couldn't wait to tell her everything. They had not been able to really spend much time together this past week and the hospital time didn't count because I had been so out of it. She had encouraged me to date Fang and had gone as far as to tell him many of my favorite things to help him out. Flipping through the channels I found one of my favorite shows. I started over with Season one of Grey's Anatomy. Sophie and I both could watch them over and over. I was on episode two when she knocked on the door and popped her head in.

"The guys are all downstairs, so Fang left the door open for me." Sophie said as she came in waving ice cream and brownies. There was a reason we were besties.

"Come on in. Please dish it up and come sit. I'm dying for some chocolate." I said as I licked my lips. She knew I loved Chocolate chip cookie dough ice cream and a warm brownie. Heaven. After fixing us both a bowl she handed me one and sat down by me on the couch. We watched for a bit while we ate and then when we finished, she rinsed the bowls and put them in the dishwasher.

"Ok, we have had dessert and tv time, now dish!" she said with her eyes twinkling. "I have been dying to know how things have been going."

"I'm sorry we haven't talked much this week. It has been insane. Things are amazing. He is sweet, sexy, caring, attentive and very thoughtful. We are moving in here together and running the business together. How crazy is that?" I said looking at my friend for support.

"It's not crazy at all. I have seen him roaming around alone. He gave up the house to his sister and Rider so they could have a home. He has been watching you for well over six months. He just got up the nerve a few months ago to start talking to you. He was so worried you wouldn't want to date someone that much older than you. I told him he was crazy that you wouldn't care. I mean, he is a great catch." Sophie said as she squeezed my hand. "He was so upset when you left the wedding. I have never seen him with her before. He doesn't bring women here. Fang and Rider are best friends and have been for years. The guys are all pretty tight."

"It's like a close-knit family that I never had. It has taken some getting used to but it's nice. I'm looking forward to the Adoption Day tomorrow even if I have to sit down and supervise rather than help." I said wistfully.

"Girl, they have gone all out. You will be blown away. They don't invite people to the property often. There will be security everywhere and all kinds of games and things going on. It will be epic." Sophie was bouncing in her seat until she saw me wince. "I'm sorry."

"I know you didn't mean to; I just can't move around much yet. I'm so sore and my meds are probably wearing off." I said, realizing how much my ribs were starting to hurt. "Can you get me some ibuprofen out of the cabinet please?"

"Didn't Doc give you some real pain medication?" she asked me as she went to look.

"He did but I know it's going to knock me out." I told her as I tried to get comfortable again. Just then the door opened, and Fang came in. He took one look at me and could tell I was hurting. Shaking his head he plucked me off the couch and carried me to the bedroom. Sophie brought my drink in with a coaster for the nightstand. She gave me a gentle hug and winked.

"Thanks, Soph, we will see you tomorrow." Fang said as he got me settled. She closed the door behind her. "I knew you wouldn't take the pain pill unless I was here to give it to you. Did you eat anything?"

I blushed as I looked at him. I nodded and swallowed the pill. "I had ice cream and brownies." He chuckled.

"It'll do." He tucked me in and kissed me. "I'll be in the other room. Holler if you need something but I expect you will probably sleep. You have a big day tomorrow. I'll be here later, baby." He stroked my hair for a few minutes until the medicine kicked in and I started to fall asleep.

15

Fang

We had all the animals cleaned and fed. They had been out for their evening walk, and we had adoption papers for all the animals prepped and ready to go. The grill was set up along with the bouncy houses, the cotton candy station and the small games. We had set up a bunch of tables under some tents near the barn and one of the local bands was set to come play. Everything was ready for the grand opening of the new Shelter and Clinic. I could not wait to see Cara's face tomorrow. The women had been cooking up a storm, making potato salad, macaroni salad, coleslaw, baked beans and all kinds of chips. It was going to be a good turnout.

Word was also spread to Freedom since they didn't have a Shelter there and Bear and his family would be coming along with some of their friends. We looked forward to seeing them. The kids were beyond excited. Cameron, Joshua, Emma and Mattie were thrilled. Now I just needed to get some sleep. I walked up the stairs to our place and went inside to shower before crawling into bed with my girl. She looked so sweet curled on her side with her fist tucked under her chin.

Doc suggested an ice pack tomorrow morning for about half an hour before we came down. I would make sure she did that as well as take a half a pill before we headed to the festivities. Crawling in bed beside her I gently eased against her back to support her and rested my hand on her hip. Closing my eyes I let myself drift off.

The next morning, she was groaning as she tried to get up. I jumped out of the bed and came around to her.

"Easy baby, let me help you. I know you need to move around to keep from getting stiff, but you're bound to be more sore today. Lean on me." She wrapped one arm through mine, and we walked slowly to the bathroom. I had removed her pants before bed last night, so she just had to raise her shirt to use the toilet. When she finished. I helped her wash her hands.

"Let's go pick out your clothes and I'll help you get dressed." I suggested. She froze.

"All my clothes are in the apartment." She looked freaked out. I shook my head and opened the closet door.

"How did you get my clothes?" Cara narrowed her eyes at me as she went to choose what she wanted to wear.

"I may have slipped Sophie your keys when you went to sleep and had her bring your stuff over." I hoped she wasn't really mad at me because I just wanted to make things easier for her.

"Oh, did she get everything?" she asked me curiously. I nodded and let out the breath I was holding. Smiling, my girl came over and crooked her finger at me. I leaned over and she kissed me silly. "I love you so much Jimmy."

"I love you too baby. I just want to make your life as easy as I can." I told her as I gently pulled her against my chest. I had to be careful not to squeeze right now. I stepped back and took the panties and jeans from her hand. "Hold on to my shoulders while I put these on you."

Once I had her dressed, we went to the kitchen, and I got her settled on the couch with some ice over her ribs. "Doc's orders." She wasn't thrilled. I made her some oatmeal and milk then put half of a pain pill beside the glass.

"I don't want to be sleepy because of this." She groaned looking at the pill by her glass.

"You won't. Doc said half would be fine but would make you more comfortable. Just no alcohol. Of course we are not having that out anyway." I told her. She finished her food and took her medicine. Looking at the time I could tell she was getting antsy to go. "How about we go on down and see the animals."

She beamed at that suggestion. I didn't tell her that we had put bows on all of them. Pink on the girls and blue on the boys. The bow also listed their names and ages. I heard a knock on the door, opening the door to see Rider standing there.

"Why don't I take the wheelchair down for you and you can grab your girl?" he suggested. Fang slapped him on the back and smiled.

"Thanks man, saves me a trip." I winked at her, and she blushed. "She will be trying to walk up and down them soon but not today. "You ready, Baby?"

"Damn straight, I want to see my babies. Where are the boys at?" she asked, looking for her dogs.

"They are down in your office. I already took them down because I knew you would want them nearby. They are wearing their collars, so people know they are not for adoption." I told her laughing.

"I'm used to them being underfoot all the time." She mumbled as I picked her up and carried her down the stairs."

"I didn't want them jumping on your ribs, you are black and blue under this shirt baby." I told her as I put her in the wheelchair. She looked around at everyone and everything with shock on her face.

"I can't believe y'all put all of this together in a few days." She stared and then looked back up at me with adoration all over her face. I melted.

"Don't you know there isn't anything I wouldn't do for you? Besides, what fun is it to have connections if you don't use them occasionally?" I said as we went to see the animals. She giggled when she saw the bows with their names and ages on them.

"Oh, my goodness, they are so cute." Cara was smiling and happy. Her eyes were shining, and I loved it. "I saw some pens outside, are those for the dogs so they can be seen by the families?"

"Yes, we figured we could bring them out a few at a time. We also have collars and leashes for purchase." I wheeled her over, so she saw what was happening outside. Tommy and Corinne along with a couple of the brothers were bringing the dogs out to put in the pen areas so the kids could see them. People were arriving and mingling. Undertaker was manning the grill with Fury. Hawk was over by the bouncy house with Cameron, Joshua, Mattie and Emma. Everyone was having a great time. There were families coming in and kids were gravitating toward the dogs. Cara was talking to a young couple who wanted one of the pit mixes. She was in her element. I had her set up at a table under an umbrella with the forms. The animals were already vaccinated and fixed. She did that as soon as she was able to. I went to fix her a drink and a plate, when I got back to her table, she was grinning from ear to ear.

"All but five of the dogs have been adopted and we only have seven cats left." Cara was beside herself, happy. Bear came over with his wife Caroline and their three girls. She was pushing them in a stroller. They were almost four years old.

"Hey Bear, long time no see." I said as I gave him a hug and then kissed Caroline on the cheek. "Look at these little beauties. You are in so much trouble."

"Yeah, I know. They can't date until they are thirty." He grumbled; the ladies laughed at him. "Who is this sweet lady over here?"

"This is my girl, Cara. She is the vet and founder of this shelter." I said proudly. "I see the girls eyeing the little fluff ball in the pink bow."

"Yeah, I guess we need to fill out the form and pay the fee. Looks like she is going home with us." Caroline kissed his cheek.

"You're a big softie." She said, smiling at him. His daughters squealed with excitement. "They have him wrapped around their little fingers."

"Well, you do too." He said as he pulled her close and kissed her forehead. Caroline blushed and went to fill out the forms and talk to Cara.

"Looks like you're having a great turnout. I think James wants to come get one of the larger dogs for Melanie. He is so paranoid about leaving her home alone." Bear chuckled as Caroline smacked his arm.

"With good reason." His wife said as she went to say hello to Annie. I watched her walk away with the kids leaving me to talk a minute.

"I'll come back for the little ball of fur before we leave." Bear said as he headed toward his family. I laughed watching him go.

"I never thought I'd see the day that he would be married with three daughters." I told Cara as she looked at the kids with a look of longing on her face. "You want kids, baby?"

"Yes, I'd love a baby eventually." She said as she watched the children playing.

16

Cara

It had been a wonderful day, all the animals got adopted so we had room to take in more from the kill shelters. We decided to wait a couple of weeks until I was healed up more. If there were any that were on the kill list, I'd send Tommy to pick them up.

I was completely exhausted but happy. Fang helped me back upstairs and put me in the bath to clean me up. He also washed my hair for me. When I got out, he helped me into one of his T-shirts, then gave me a pain pill and put me to bed. I hoped the next few weeks went quickly because I wanted to be intimate with him and I couldn't. That was going to drive me nuts. He fixed me a drink to put by the bed and crawled in with me. Spock and Kirk jumped up and laid by my feet as usual. We were asleep in no time.

I woke up to Fang talking on the phone, I glanced at the clock. It was three in the morning. He sounded upset so I turned on the lamp on my side of the bed and waited for him to finish his conversation. When he hung up, he looked wrecked. I put my hand on his back and rubbed it.

"What's wrong honey?" I asked him quietly. He turned and looked at me then leaned over and kissed my lips hungrily. I put my hands on either side of his face and held him to me for a minute. "Baby, tell me what's going on."

"Gears' sister, Dawn, is missing. She is a law student at Berkeley and there have been several girls who have come missing lately. Her roommate called Gears and said that they were at the party, and she was just gone. She thought at first, she had left with someone but when tried to call her she found Dawn's phone in a trash can outside the frat house. She knew the police would not do anything anytime soon, so she called Gears immediately. There are sex trafficking rings around there and we are sending a team in to find her. She has a GPS tracker in all her jewelry. We have a location for her, and we leave within the hour. I hate to go but she is family. Gears is going to, so Sophie is going to come stay with you while we are gone." Fang looked at me and I knew he hated to leave me. I refused to make him feel bad for doing his job.

"I understand, please let me know you're okay when you can. I'll miss you. I love you so much." I said as I tugged on his arm to kiss him again. "I'm guessing that's what the packed duffle in the closet is for. A go, bag?"

"You are so smart and yes, we all keep one ready." He said as he caressed my face. "Be safe, don't overdo it, be careful going up and down the stairs. I wish I had put in a fucking elevator."

I chuckled at him. I sent him the picture of us from the wedding to his phone. He looked down and smiled at me.

"I have to go but hopefully we will have Dawn and be home in a couple days." He said as he got up threw on some clothes and then came over and tucked me back in. "Go back to sleep baby."

"I'll try, be safe." I said as I watched him go. A few minutes later Sophie came in and crawled in bed with me. She would probably sleep in the guest room tomorrow but wanted me to know she was here. The dogs just moved over closer to me.

"They will be fine; this is what they really do. Go back to sleep and they will let us know when we get there." Sophie mumbled before turning over and burying her face in the covers. I had moved over to have his pillow, so she was on my side now. I laid awake until my alarm went off at five. I knew her phone was set for six. I eased out of bed and put on panties then went to start the coffee. I couldn't believe this was my new home. It was more than twice as big as the apartment I had. I opened the fridge and clearly someone had gone shopping for us. I went back to get dressed and brush my teeth. My hair I just threw into a ponytail. Then I went to get a cup of coffee and make some toast. I would try to just take some Tylenol today. I kept my phone on the charger and made sure my volume was up so that I would hear if he called. When Sophie's alarm went off, she stumbled in for coffee. I handed her a cup; made it the way she liked it. Then she went to get dressed. After the toast was done, I put some on her plate and a couple on mine. I pulled out the peanut butter because we both liked it on our toast.

"So, I will help you downstairs after I take the dogs down to your office. Then I'll head to work. Undertaker will be around as well as Hawk, Remy and Luke. Gears, Fang, Axle, Blade, Rider and Fury went along with Doc. He will be there in case she needs medical attention or any of the guys need it. I'll call you at lunch. You can send Tommy to pick up lunch or one of the guys will probably bring something by." Sophie finished her breakfast and put her dishes and mine in the dishwasher. "Ok boys, who wants to go outside."

The boys came barking to the door and waited. They made the stairs with two landings so they would be wider and safer for the dogs and myself. Sophie opened the door, and they ran out to go. Once she got them secured in my office, she came back up to walk down with me. Once I got settled into my office she headed to work, and I started doing paperwork from the event yesterday. Thankfully my client list was online so I started to call everyone and leave voicemails letting them know our new address and to call and reschedule their pets appointments. My phone rang around nine-thirty, it was Fang letting me know they were there and safe for now. He said he would try to actually call me tonight. I told him I loved him and to be careful. I sent Sophie a text that I heard from him, and she replied that she had as well. I looked over the schedule and was satisfied that I had a full schedule for the next few weeks. I was letting Tommy take what he could, and I am just taking the ones he can't do.

The day went by pretty quickly. Hawk had dropped off some lunch for me and checked to make sure I was doing okay. I had come into my office this morning to find a gift basket from Fang with a huge 40 oz tumbler that was pink and said Dog Mom on it. It was adorable, there were also some chocolates and protein bars along with a cute coffee mug for my desk. I walked to the back to let my dogs in the yard to do their business and feed them. Fang had bought them both beds to put in my office by the window. They also had new toys. He was the sweetest man.

Sophie messaged me about four-thirty to let me know she was on her way back. I did my best to take it easy today. Since we didn't have any surrenders today it was a light day for me.

17

Fang

We got Dawn's phone from her roommate. Gears had told her if she ever felt uncomfortable or unsafe to turn it on video so it would also record voices. We were going over the phone listening and watching the last video. We heard some Russian voices in the background and Dawn screaming out descriptions of them and their vehicles. We set up in her dorm and Gears started to hack into the video traffic cams to see what he could find. We had a MC in that area that we were friendly with. They were checking to see what they could find as well. Gears was normally really laid back and easygoing but it you messed with his family or his woman he could be a mean, nasty fucker with a knife. He had no mercy for people who hurt women, children or animals. We were all like that.

I glanced over and saw a picture of Gears, Sophie and Dawn from Christmas over a year ago. It was sweet that she kept it out. They had always been close, and they talked all the time. Gears was a ticking time bomb. I just prayed that we found her in one piece and alive or he would lose his damn mind. Doc was very agitated as well. I knew he had a soft spot for Dawn, but he seemed to look at her differently the last time she was home. He was pacing around the room as well.

"Got it, they are about three blocks from the closest airfield in a hangar. I was able to find a camera feed that they must not realize is still active. Looks like there are only a couple of guards outside. There is a van and a jeep parked in front. We have infrared cameras, and we will leave in twenty minutes. The other MC is going to back us up. They are pretty pissed about the sex trafficking especially in their city. They have the place surrounded. Let's get going. I want my fucking sister home where she belongs. She can finish school online." Gears got up and strapped his guns and his knives. He had on his beanie he always wore and looked load for bear.

We drove around the back of the airfield where the local MC told us to park so we would not be seen going in. It was completely dark, and we were all armed and ready with smoke bombs and tear gas. Our masks were on, and we moved in. Doc was in the van waiting. Axle and Blade took out the two guards with silencers, while Fury and Rider went in from the back. Gears and I took the front. There were only four guards inside. One in the can, one standing by the front door, one by the back door and one balls deep in one of the girls. If it was Dawn, he was going to die. We tossed a smoke bomb inside and went in, taking the one at the door first then the one in the bathroom. Fury and Rider took out the two in the back. We opened the windows to air out the gas.

There were six women in the cages and one that was curled into a ball on the floor. We made our way in and unlocked the cages, releasing the girls. We just wanted to find Dawn, the local MC would take care of the rest of them.

"Dawn, baby girl, where are you?" Gears shouted as he looked at the girls to find his sister.

"Austin?" the girl in the corner sobbed. Damn, she was the one being raped. Gears went over to her and wrapped a blanket around her shoulders picking her up.

"Yes, baby sister, it's me. You're safe now. I'm so sorry I didn't get here in time." He carried her out to the van to Doc. There were tears in his eyes when he looked at her torn dress and the blood on her thighs. There was nothing left of the men in the hangar because we couldn't take a chance of them alerting any backup. The guys gave blankets to the other girls, and we took them all to the van to be checked over. Doc gave them all bottles of water, and I radioed the president of the local club to come get the others and take them to the hospital. Doc was looking over Dawn, cleaning her up and bandaging her scraps. He wrapped her in a clean blanket and held her in his lap. She clung to him shaking like a leaf. Gears was sitting beside them looking helpless.

We loaded up and headed to the plane we had chartered. The other guys would pick up the van after we left. When we boarded the plane Gears tried to take Dawn from Doc, but she wasn't having it. She wouldn't let go of his shirt.

"I've got her. You know I won't hurt her." Doc said gruffly as he said on the couch and buckled them in together. He had the blanket around her and was gently rocking her and singing to her. She finally went limp in his arms, and he knew she had passed out from sheer exhaustion. Gears sat in the chair closest to them. I sent a message to Cara that we had her and were on our way home. I also told her to let Sophie know that Dawn was in bad shape and therefore Gears was going to be on a hair trigger to just be patient with him.

"I let the girls know we were on our way home. You may want to shoot yours a quick message." I told Gears. He nodded and pulled his phone out and typed a message then put it back in his pocket and just stared at his baby sister. Knowing she was the one being assaulted when we arrived was fucking with his head. We would need to get her some counseling.

The plane took off for home and we were all silent on the way back. We were thankful to find her alive, but she was not unharmed. That hit home for all of us. We had not slept in over thirty-six hours, and we were all dragging. I had a feeling that Gears was going to want to take Dawn home with him, but Doc was not going to let that happen. When we arrived at the airstrip outside of town, we disembarked and got into our own vehicles. Doc had the Medi-van parked there so he loaded Dawn in the back on the gurney. He wanted to give her something for the pain and to help her sleep, but he didn't know if she had been drugged. When we got home, they parked by Doc's house, and he carried Dawn inside with Gears hot on his heels. Axle and I followed them in to keep the peace.

"She needs to go home with me, Doc." Gears said as he tried to reach for her. Doc stepped in front of him. Axle and Blade back him up.

"I am keeping her here for observation. I'll need to do an examination on her to see how badly she was hurt and find out if they drugged her. If not, I can administer an antibiotic and some pain medication. It's easier if I administer it through an IV. She is obviously comfortable with me, and I don't want to take her to the hospital unless I have to. You are welcome to come by in the morning to check on her." Doc was trying to be as gentle about it as he could. When he started to put her back down, she whimpered and clung to him. "I need to get her settled and we all need some sleep. I'll be in the chair by her bed tonight."

"Fine, I'll be back tomorrow to check on her." Gears said as he left. I followed him to my place, and he came up to get Sophie. I unlocked the door, and my girl was asleep on the couch with Sophie on the other side. Gears went over and kissed Sophie.

"Baby, let's go home." He whispered to her. Her bag was beside the couch, so he slung it over his shoulder, and they left. I picked up my girl and carried her to our bed. I stripped off my clothes and took a quick shower then crawled in beside her.

18

Cara

I was so relieved to get the call from Fang about Dawn. Knowing they were on the way home helped me to sleep. I just didn't want to sleep in our bed without him. I knew he was home when I felt myself being carried to bed. When he laid me down, I expected him to climb in after, but I heard the shower come on in our bathroom. I made myself stay awake until he got into bed beside me. I wanted to feel his arms around me as I went back to sleep.

A few minutes later I felt the bed move and he spooned me from behind. I settled as soon as I felt him surrounding me.

"I love you so much baby girl." He whispered in my ear as he kissed my cheek. "Go back to sleep, we will talk in the morning."

The next morning, we got up and I got ready for work. I was starting to move around a little better but very sore and I had to take it slowly. He went and took the dogs outside while I fixed some breakfast. When he came back in, they were already down in my office. We sat down to eat, and he sipped on his coffee quietly.

"How is Dawn?" I asked him, knowing that was on his mind. "I'm so glad that you found her. She must have been so scared."

"Honey, Dawn was being raped when we arrived. She is at Doc's place. Gears are taking this really hard. He feels like he should have made her attend school here." Fang ate a few bites, but I could tell he didn't have much of an appetite. "She seems to feel safe with Doc so he insisted she stay with him so he can take care of her. It's going to be a bit tense for a while."

"Oh, poor thing, that's so horrible. She is going to need counseling." I told him as I took our plates and dumped the rest of our food. Neither of us could eat right now.

Fang got up and put his arms around me from behind, gently holding me close to him. I felt him tremble and placed my hands over his hands. My guy could be so tough, but he was also a gentle soul.

"I hope he's dead." I said quietly. "I wish he could have suffered but I just want her to know he is dead and won't be coming back for her."

"My bloodthirsty little girl. Yes, all of them are dead and the MC in the area will hunt down whoever wasn't there." He told me. "Let's get you to work and I have to go debrief. I also want to go check on Dawn."

"Okay honey." I said as I got my purse and slipped on my shoes. We walked down to the Clinic, and I saw Gears walking over towards Doc's place. He looked so distraught. "He is going to need counseling too."

"Yeah, I just hope we get him to go." Fang said, frowning. He walked me to my office and then pulled me into his arms and kissed me. "Don't overdo it, I'll be back, and I will bring lunch.

"Okay honey." I said as I locked my purse in my drawer and pulled up my calendar for the day.

I watched him leave and thought about how lucky I was to have such a wonderful guy. I knew he had to do bad things to save people sometimes, but I was okay with that. I knew I would never be safer than if I was with him.

Lunch rolled around and my guy came in with a pizza. I already had two patients today and I had three more appointments. I was slowly getting back to work and making sure I didn't overdo it. I will add to it over the next few weeks. Tommy was asking for more hours and since I didn't have to dip into my insurance money, I would be able to afford that. It also meant we could start taking more walk-ins. He was almost done with school and interning with me. I wanted to keep him on and as business picks up, hire someone to work at the reception desk. We only had one other vet in town.

"Are you ready for lunch baby?" Fang asked me as he pulled up a chair and fixed our plates. He also brought some dog treats for Spock and Kirk. They both loved fresh carrots, so he had picked up some of the cut-up kind.

"This looks good. How is Dawn?" I asked as I took a bite of my pizza. "I'd like to cook dinner for Gears and Sophie soon. Have them over to our place."

"That would be nice. As far as Dawn is concerned, she will be staying at Doc's for a while. She is not really talking right now, and every time Gears suggested taking her home with him, she got agitated. She seems to have some kind of close bond with Doc. Gears is a bit miffed by that and has questions but for now, Doc is the best person to care for her. He is the only person she lets near her." Fang took another slice of pizza.

"Does she like animals?" I asked him as I took a drink. He nodded and sat back in his chair. "I got a call about some kittens that will be weaned soon. They can't keep them. The mother will be spayed as soon as she is healed. I thought I would bring one over for her or take Kirk over to see her. Sometimes animals are really good company for trauma victims."

"That would be nice, baby." He said as he cleaned up our lunch. "I am going to go clean the kennels and get ready for the kittens and then maybe drive around to see if there are any strays that need care. I'll be back before dinner time."

"You are such a softie Jimmy Watson." I said and got up to sit in his lap. "I love you and I can't wait to be your wife. I don't want a big wedding and I don't want to wait."

He looked up at me in surprise and his face lit up. I put my arms around his neck and kissed him. A minute later we heard the buzzer for the front door. I blushed and got up.

"That is probably my next patient. I'll see you at home later." I smiled at him and went back to work.

When I had finished my last appointment of the day, I looked up to see Doc in the doorway. He looked exhausted.

"Hey Cara, I thought I would come check your ribs." He said as he pointed to one of my exam rooms. I followed him in and closed the door.

"You look beat. Have you slept at all?" I asked him knowingly. He shook his head. "You won't be able to properly take care of Dawn if you don't take care of yourself."

"I know, I just kept seeing her when they brought her out to the van last night. It was horrible. I have seen a lot in the emergency room, but it's different when it's someone you know and care about." He said as he raised my shirt up. "Hold your shirt under your breasts, I just want to see how your ribs are feeling." He gently pressed around, and I winced. "Sorry, I know it's bruised and tender. I brought some arnica for you to put on them to help." He pulled a bottle out of his coat pocket and handed it to me. "Make sure you are careful going up and down those stairs."

"I will, you go get some rest. Grab a baby monitor so you can hear her if she wakes up or roll a cot in the room and sleep there, but you have to get some rest." I fussed at him. He looked at me ruefully and shook his head.

"You are going to be a great mom someday. You already have the mother hen thing down pat." I stuck my tongue out at him as he chuckled and left. I heard Fang greet him as he was leaving.

"Hey baby, what did Doc say?" he asked as he looked at my ribs and bent to press kisses on them.

"He said it looks about how he expected and just not to overdo it. He also brought something to help with the bruising. Let's go home, I just want to eat a light dinner and cuddle with my guy." I whistled for my dogs and we all went upstairs to our place.

19

D awn

I was crouched in a cage trying to make myself invisible. I knew what happened when they let one of us out. They didn't even bother to take us to a separate room. They just pulled a girl out, drugged her then ripped her clothes off and raped her right on the table. Sometimes it was just one man, sometimes two or three. They would laugh and say they were breaking us in for our new lives in a Russian brothel. I was pretty sure I had only been here a couple of days, but it felt longer. They barely gave us anything to drink and had only tossed us packets of peanut butter crackers to eat. I could hear the girls crying and when one was being used, we all heard the screams. I was terrified of it being my turn. I was a virgin. It wasn't that I hadn't dated but no one made me feel like I wanted that. At least no one but Dr. Cole Harper, road name Doc. I had a crush on him for years, but he didn't notice me until the last time was home for a visit.

I heard the door creak open and one of the men came in. I glanced toward the door, and it was the mean one. He had been eyeing me since I got here. Suddenly my cage door opened, and he grabbed me out. I tried to fight but I was so weak from lack of food and being bent over for so long. He punched me in the face and then flipped me on my stomach and ripped my pants down. I felt him spit and shove his cock into me. I felt myself tearing and I cried. It hurt so badly, he kept going until suddenly I heard a shot, and he slipped out and fell. I crouched down in the corner as far away as I could get. There was a lot of commotion going on and suddenly I heard my brother's voice.

I woke up in a cold sweat. Jerking up from the bed. Cole was there beside me and he gently sat down and held me while I cried. He has not left my side since they saved me. I just wish they had been about half an hour sooner. I calmed down and turned over facing away from him. I hated that he was seeing me like this. I just wanted to die.

"Baby girl, I know you have a lot to work through. I just want you to know you can stay with me as long as you need to. I'll take care of you." Doc whispered as he gently wiped my face with a cool damp cloth. I heard him leave the room quietly and I just stared out the window.

The End.

- SAMHSA'S (Substance Abuse and Mental Health Services Administration) National Helpline, 1-800-662-HELP (4357). (also known as the Treatment Referral Routing Service), or TTY: 1-800-487-4889 is a confidential, free 24-hour-a-day, 365-day a-year information service, in English and Spanish, for individuals and family members facing mental and/or substance use disorders. This service provides referrals to local treatment facilities, support groups, and community-based organizations.

- Also visit the online treatment locator or send your zip code via text message: 435748 (HELP4U) to find help near you.

-

- *I have included this information as a way to hopefully reach out to those in need. My daughter is an addict, I pray for her every day that she will get help. She has lost many friends to suicide and overdose. If this helps anyone then it is worth it.*

-

-

Made in United States
Troutdale, OR
05/17/2024

19937026R00056